IN PURSUIT

OF THE

GIANT SABLE

ANTELOPE

IN PURSUIT

OF THE

GIANT SABLE

ANTELOPE

JOHN MANUEL

atmosphere press

© 2024 John Manuel

Published by Atmosphere Press

Cover design by Kevin Stone

No part of this book may be reproduced without permission from the author except in brief quotations and in reviews. This is a work of fiction, and any resemblance to real places, persons, or events is entirely coincidental.

Atmospherepress.com

*In memory of Quentin Keynes,
the man who first took me to Africa*

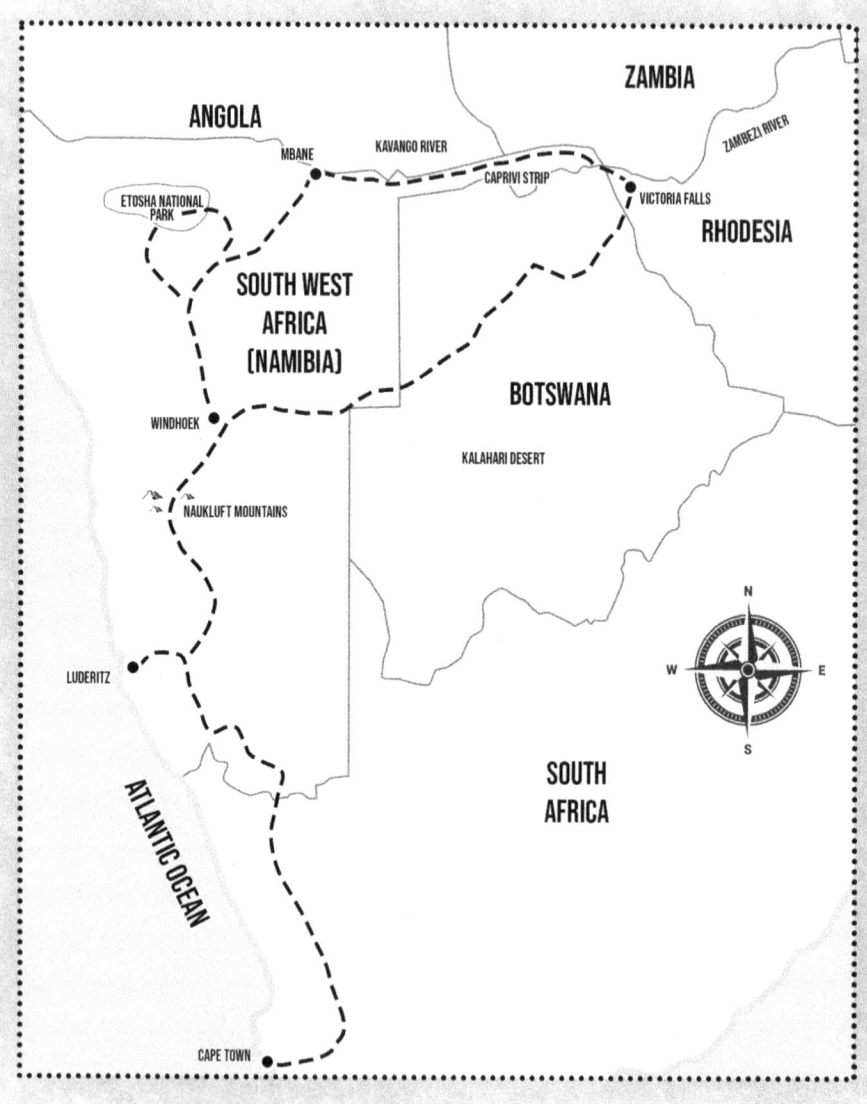

WALKER'S JOURNEY, 1975

Chapter 1

Walker Scoville stood atop the gangway of the SS *Edinburgh Castle*, shivering in the predawn darkness. Somewhere out there lay the City of Cape Town and beyond it, the whole of Africa. What was this chuffing coming from the docks? It sounded like a steam engine, but this was 1975, and steam locomotives were twenty years gone from the States. A plume of white flashed against the void. It *was* a steam engine, a fire-breathing dragon, stalking the railyard!

"Yes, they still use them here," someone said. "Price of oil and all."

Beyond the railyard, the city began to emerge—white buildings sloping to the base of the massive, flat-topped Table Mountain. A sliver of sunlight gilded the mountain's crest and like a curtain, slid downward until the flank glowed orange across the horizon.

A whistle sounded. Cecil Covington, leader of Walker's group of five, turned toward his American charges.

"Time to walk the plank," he said. "Isn't this fantastic!"

Alec Chapman did not react. A head taller and, at eighteen, a year older than Walker, Alec seemed to take everything at a cool remove. Walker hoped Alec would open up over the course of the trip, but if not he would live with it. Walker's friend, Paul Schwartz, was another matter. At the sound of the whistle, Schwartzy leaped onto the ship's railing and aimed his Nikon camera at the unfolding city.

A deck officer shouted. "You there! Down, now!"

Schwartzy took two more shots, then scrambled back in line.

A voice deadpanned in Walker's ear. "Our house monkey strikes again." Chas Morgan, smart, glib, brushed a lock of red hair from his eye. Chas usually made Walker laugh, but his cynicism was not appreciated today. Not with the wonder that Walker was feeling.

Elliot Stroud stretched on his tiptoes, his boyish face rising behind Chas's. "What's happening, guys? Can you see?" Elliot was the smallest and, at age fifteen, the youngest of the group. His neediness bothered Walker, but he was otherwise tolerable.

"You'll see in a minute," Walker said.

He reached the gangway and started down. It had been twelve days since he'd last felt solid ground, six thousand miles from Southampton to Cape Town. He stepped off the gangway and onto the pavement.

"God, this feels weird," he said to Schwartzy. "No rocking."

Schwartzy waved his hands in the air. "Dude, we're here!"

The line moved a dozen yards and stalled in front of a low brick building emblazoned with the words "Customs House." Walker unshouldered his duffle bag and turned to take a last look at the *Edinburg Castle*. She was an impressive ship—eight hundred feet long and five stories tall, but Cecil said she would soon be retired, a victim of air travel.

He took out his camera and snapped a photo.

"Alright, boys, we're moving," Cecil said.

They passed through a set of glass double doors and up to the first desk. Cecil presented his British passport to the agent, a burly White man in a blue short-sleeved shirt.

"Goeiedag," the agent said.

What was this, Afrikaans, the bastardized version of Dutch used by the descendants of South Africa's first White settlers? Why would the agent use that language and not English? He perused Cecil's passport.

"Been here quite a few times, Mr. Covington. What's your business?"

"I bring boys here on safari," Cecil said. "Been doing it every year since 1960."

"Will you be traveling out of South Africa?"

"Yes, to South West."

That would be South West Africa, a former German colony, now under the control of South Africa.

"Botswana and Rhodesia, as well," Cecil added.

The itinerary didn't seem to bother the agent. He stamped the passport and handed it back.

Alec was next in line. The agent flipped through his passport and asked him what he'd been doing in France.

"It was my junior year abroad," Alec said.

"Travel to any other countries while you were there?"

"No, sir."

The agent turned the pages back and forth as if they would reveal something treacherous about this eighteen-year-old prep schooler.

"Next."

Walker presented his passport, expecting to be asked about his travel to Mexico. Instead, the agent fixated on his photo. What was the problem? His shoulder-length hair?

"Where will you be staying in Cape Town?" the agent said.

"I don't know. I'm with Mr. Covington."

"You don't know where you're staying?"

"No, sir."

A long pause. This asshole clearly enjoyed watching him sweat. Whack! The stamp came down.

At the next station, a pair of agents rummaged through the boys' duffle bags. One of them held aloft a paperback, *Catch 22*.

"Whose is this?"

Elliot raised his hand. "Mine."

The agent tossed the book into a wastebasket. "Prohibited."

"Sir, that's my summer reading!" Elliot said.

"It's prohibited."

The agent pulled out two other books—*1984* and *Fahrenheit 451*—and tossed them out as well. Elliot, close to tears, turned to Walker.

"Now what am I going to do? I'll never have time to read them before school starts."

Walker shrugged. He could only guess at the reasons for the books being banned—questioning of authority, fear of anti-war sentiment corroding South African society? His duffle bag came next. Two of his books—*Slaughterhouse-Five* and *The Autobiography of Malcolm X*—were bound to raise suspicion. Sure enough, the agent tossed them in the wastebasket. A third book, *The Essays of Henry D. Thoreau*, gave the man pause. He studied the cover, checked some list, and then returned it to the duffle. Apparently, Thoreau was not a sufficient threat to the rule of law in South Africa.

Outside the Customs House, Cecil stood waiting.

"What on earth took you so long?" he said.

"They confiscated my summer reading books!" Elliot said.

Cecil shook his head. "Stupid Afrikaners."

Here was more evidence of the cultural divide. The English considered themselves superior to the Afrikaners. No surprise there. And more liberal. But the limits of that distinction were soon born out. A taxi pulled to the curb, its top light read "Whites Only."

Schwartzy scowled. "What is this? Some apartheid bullshit?"

"Don't make trouble," Cecil said. "You're not in America anymore."

"I'm not taking this cab."

"Just get in." Cecil all but shoved Walker and Schwartzy into the back seat while directing Alec, Chas, and Elliot to take the next cab. He climbed into the front seat and gave directions to the driver. "Queen Elizabeth Guesthouse," he said. "It's on Kloof Street."

"Yis, I know whey eet ees," the driver said.

It took Walker a moment to piece together the accent. R's were pronounced as A's, and I's as E's.

"Come off the *Castle*, did you?" the driver said.

"Yes," Cecil said. "Quite a long journey."

"All the way from England?"

"These boys came from America. They flew to London and we took the ship from there."

The driver glanced in the rearview mirror. "We don't see many Yanks these days. Politics and all."

Walker wondered about that. A fair number of his parent's friends had been to Africa, but always to East

Africa—Kenya, Uganda, Tanzania. Those countries were famous for their wildlife, but maybe politics had something to do with it.

Through the open window, he took in the sights and smells of Cape Town. Beyond the railyard with its primitive steam engines and drab box cars lay a modern city—glass office towers mixed with two- and three-story shops painted in pastels and whites. The sidewalks appeared clean and were filled with pedestrians—Asian, Black, Colored, and White. Black men, he noted, were well dressed in button-down shirts and slacks, women in colorful dresses.

The Queen Elizabeth Guest House was a modest affair—a stucco building in need of a new coat of paint. Walker lugged his duffle bag up the steps and crowded with the others into the small reception area. The desk clerk checked them in and led them down the hall.

"I can put three in here," she said. "Two single beds and a roll out."

Cecil stuck his head in. "Yes, this will do. Walker, Chas, Paul, why don't you take this one?"

The three boys stepped inside and closed the door. Schwartzy tested the springs on one of the beds.

"Cecil sure pinched his pennies with this place," he said. "Brits are such skinflints."

"Yeah, that's probably why we went by ship," Walker said. "Cheaper than flying, at least the way we went—second class. Or was it third?"

"I don't think money was his primary motivation for going by ship," Chas said. "I think he fancies himself an old-time explorer. The David Livingstone of the 1970s."

"Why do you say that?" Walker said.

"Because I read his journal."

"He's keeping a journal? He never showed me anything."

"He kept it in his cabin," Chas said. "I found it open on his desk."

"You broke into his room?"

"The door was unlocked."

Walker was shocked at Chas's behavior. But he was curious about this journal.

"So, what did it say?" he asked.

Chas flipped his hair from his brow and took on a theatrical voice. "*On day six, we crossed the equator. The seas were calm. No sign yet of the continent...*"

Schwartzy laughed, but Walker found it intriguing. Cecil had been to Africa more than a dozen times, but he still saw it as a grand adventure. A sixty-year-old man filled with boyish enthusiasm. You had to admire that.

Nine months earlier, Walker and Schwartzy sat together in the dining hall at Choate, the prep school they attended in Wallingford, Connecticut. The last Friday of each month, the school invited a guest speaker, and today's guest was a man whom the headmaster described as "a modern-day African explorer." Up to the microphone stepped a six-foot-three, stoop-shouldered Englishman with narrow-set eyes and jumbled teeth. He began by saying he'd fallen in love with Africa as a boy, reading the accounts of John Hanning Speke, David Livingstone, and Sir Richard Burton.

"I shan't dare say I'm the equal of any of them, but I love exploring the remote corners of the continent," Cecil said. "I make films of all my trips, and I've got one today I think you'll enjoy."

The headmaster turned off the lights and switched on the projector. The film had no soundtrack, but Cecil narrated it in a riveting voice. Here stood a huge bull elephant, staring right at the camera, ears flared wide.

"This was in Botswana," Cecil said. "One of the largest elephants I've ever seen."

The animal raised its trunk, pinpointing the intruder by smell. Then, he charged. Walker felt a surge of adrenaline. Look out! Run! The elephant skidded to a halt in a cloud of dust. Guffaws of amazement filled the auditorium.

"A close call, that!" Cecil said.

Walker shook his head. How did Cecil know the elephant would stop? This man had balls. Or else he was a fool.

The film jumped to a shot of an albino giraffe peering over the top of an acacia tree.

"Rarely seen, mind you," Cecil said. "I may have the only shot of this particular animal."

On he went through scenes of African natives pounding drums, a double rainbow in front of an enormous waterfall, and diminutive Bushmen crowding around a Land Rover. The film was not particularly well-edited, nothing like you'd see on TV, but what experiences this man had!

When the lights came on, Cecil entertained questions. Walker was the first to raise his hand. Did he ever take anyone with him on his trips?

"Yes, I take six or seven boys every year," Cecil said. "Ones I've chosen carefully, mind you. If you're interested, come see me afterwards."

He looked at Schwartzy. "Let's check it out."

Up on stage, the two of them expressed their desire to learn more about these trips. Cecil asked why they were particularly interested in Africa. For Walker, it was the wildlife. He was fascinated with African animals, and not just the obvious ones—the lions, and elephants, and rhinoceros. He loved the antelopes with their myriad shaped horns, the crazy colored birds, the lizards, and snakes. Schwartzy expressed an interest in African culture—the many tribes with their unique clothing and masks. But would they be willing, Cecil wondered, to spend a month and a half in the bush, sleeping on the ground, eating canned food? Yes, they'd both gone to summer camps where those things were routine.

Cecil nodded. "Do either of you happen to live nearby?"

"I do," Walker said. "Paul's a boarder."

"Would your parents mind if I spent the night? I've not booked a hotel room just yet."

Walker hesitated. He'd never had a stranger ask to spend the night in his parents' house. And he wasn't on particularly good terms with them, the result of his "too close" relationship with an "undesirable" girlfriend. But he'd do whatever was necessary to accommodate Cecil.

"Let me call them," he said. "I think they'd be happy to have you."

Cecil ended up spending two nights at the Scovilles' instead of one. Walker suspected the man had never intended to stay in a hotel, but he won his parents over with infectious enthusiasm. He sang the praises of the Scoville house with its view of the Housatonic River. He complimented Walker's father for his excellent library—"I'm a bit of a book collector myself"—and his mother for her wide selection of tea.

At one point, Walker's father asked Cecil if he was married.

"Goodness, no," Cecil laughed. "I couldn't have a wife the way I live. I'm traveling four months of the year, you see."

This sounded reasonable to Walker and seemed to satisfy his father.

The last night, sipping his tea in the living room, Cecil announced that he would be delighted to take Walker with him to Africa. He presented Walker's father with a sheet of paper listing the price. Walker's father took time to respond.

"I could come down a bit on the price if necessary," Cecil said.

"Thank you, but that's not the issue," his father said. He glanced at Walker. "We'll talk this over and get back to you."

After settling into the Queen Elizabeth Guest House, Cecil called the boys to his room. He needed to retrieve two Land Rovers he kept at a garage in Cape Town. Alec, the only other member of the group old enough to hold an international driver's license, would need to come with him. Alec would be driving the second Land Rover for the entirety of the trip.

"The rest of you are free to go downtown," Cecil said. "Be sure to drop your parents a postcard to let them know you've arrived. And don't eat too big a lunch. We've been invited to a friend's house for dinner."

They set off on foot, passing among ever taller buildings and crowded sidewalks. Many of the people were Africans, well-dressed and going about their business. It seemed the races could coexist in a public space. So why the need for these apartheid rules?

They stopped in front of a shop with an array of African-themed curios displayed on the sidewalk. Elliot picked up a carved giraffe, one of a dozen set in a line.

"This looks pretty nice," he said.

Chas took it from him. "This is just tourist shlock," he said. "I bet you'll find the exact same thing in every craft store."

He handed it back and stared down the street. "I wonder if there's a place in this town that sells girly mags. Who wants to come with me?"

"I guess I will," Elliot said.

Walker and Schwartzy entered the store and started down the aisle. Walker picked up a wooden bust of an African woman in traditional head garb. He thought it nicely executed, but he wondered if, as Chas suggested, it was mass-produced. At the end of the aisle, he paused in front of a map of the U.S. tacked to the wall. It was titled *Indian Battles of the American West.* He looked closer. Here in red ink were the names of dozens of battles, with a one- or two-sentence descriptor listing the number of American soldiers killed versus the number of Indians. Some, like the Battle of Little Bighorn, were known to him, but others were not. Where had they gotten this map, and why was it displayed in this store?

"Schwartzy, come look at this map. It celebrates American victories over the Indians."

Schwartzy walked over. "Wow. Never seen anything like this. And you wouldn't these days. Not in the States."

"This must be how the South Africans see themselves. Surrounded by Indians."

"And, boy, do they wish things would turn out for them like they did for us."

"How do you mean?"

"We killed most of the Indians first, then stuck the survivors on reservations. We cut the population down to where they wouldn't pose a threat."

True. Maybe, then, White Americans weren't that different from White South Africans. It was a disturbing thought and one that Walker quickly dismissed. He circled around to the front of the store and thumbed through a rack of postcards. Here was a nice photo of Table Mountain in the morning sunlight, the same view he saw from the ship. He bought it, asking the clerk where the nearest post office was. The man pointed out the window to the far side of the square. "Right there."

He and Schwartzy sat in the shade of a leafy tree and scribbled notes to their parents. "Dear Mom and Dad, I have arrived safely after a long and pretty boring cruise. Cape Town is beautiful, and my tripmates seem pretty nice. I hope you have a nice trip to France. Love, Walker."

They approached the post office, a handsome granite-clad building with two entrances. One bearing the word "Whites Only" had no line. The other marked "Non-Whites" had a long line of patrons. Most were dark-skinned, but there were lighter-skinned Indians, as well.

Schwartzy shook his head. "This is fucked up. Come on, Walker, let's get in the Non- Whites line."

Walker hesitated. "I don't know if that's a good idea."

"Come on, man!"

He trailed Schwartzy to the back of the line. Immediately, the Black man in front of them grew agitated. He pointed to the Whites Only entrance.

"You are supposed to be over there," he said.

"Hey, man, we're cool," Schwartzy said.

"No, you must go over there!"

"Come on, Schwartzy," Walker said. "They don't want trouble. You heard what Cecil said."

Back at the guest house, they found Cecil standing beside a red Land Rover, an agitated look on his face.

"Have any of you seen Alec?" he said.

The boys shook their heads.

"He was supposed to follow me in the other Land Rover. He was right behind me at the start."

"Maybe he got lost," Schwartzy said.

"He's got the address. There's no excuse for getting lost."

Twenty minutes later, Alec appeared driving a blue Land Rover. He stepped out, looking perfectly calm.

Cecil upbraided him. "Where the hell have you been? I've been waiting almost half an hour."

"I had trouble with the gears. I couldn't get it into second."

"I told you that you have to double clutch between first and second. You were right behind me for a while. I thought you had it down."

"Not quite."

"Are you going to be able to drive, or do I need to give you a lesson?"

"I figured it out."

"I certainly hope so. I can't have you falling behind."

Chapter 2

Cecil squeezed behind the desk in his second-class stateroom aboard the *Edinburg Castle*, drew the book out of his suitcase, and carefully opened it. The leather cover crackled as he pressed it flat, the smell of that ancient goatskin filling him with joy. Cecil was a collector of books by and about the great nineteenth-century African explorers, and this was one of his treasures—a first edition of David Livingstone's *Expedition to the Zambesi and Its Tributaries*, published in 1866. One might consider him a fool for bringing such a rarity on his trip, but he dared not leave it at his flat in London, which could easily be robbed. And, too, being able to read the very words of this great explorer as he, Cecil, drew near the Dark Continent made his journey seem all the more special.

Since his youth, Cecil had dreamed of being an explorer in the mold of Burton, Speke, and Livingstone. He was a member of the Royal Geographic Society in London and longed to be ranked among its notables. But by the 1960s, there was little of Africa left to be explored. Every river's source was known, every country mapped. Parts of the Belgian Congo might yet be untrammeled by Whites, but he lacked the stamina or the finances to go tramping through the jungle. So he contented himself with seeking out the odd spectacle—an albino giraffe in Kenya, the wreckage of a World War II German bomber in the Namib Desert.

His presentations were a hit with audiences in the U.S.—prep schools and natural history museums—but the Royal Geographic Society was a tough sell. The stuffed shirts sat through the films stone-faced, questioning him afterward as to whether he was really the first to film that bomber. And didn't Sir Reginald have a shot of an albino elephant? Their reaction hurt him deeply. Every discovery he made, they considered trivial, all his hard-won footage, the work of an amateur. But he had one ace up his sleeve, and at age sixty, with his physical abilities starting to decline, it was time to go for it.

He leafed through the pages of Livingstone's book to his description of his 1875 exploration of Victoria Falls. Livingstone was one of the first White men ever to see the falls, and the local Makololo tribesman insisted on giving him the best view by transporting him to an island in the Zambezi River at the very edge of the falls. His description was thrilling, but there was something else that, in Cecil's mind, was equally memorable.

"With considerable trepidation, I boarded one of their canoes, which they expertly paddled to the upstream end of the island," Livingstone wrote. *"We proceeded to walk through dense forest, the thundering sound of falling water growing ever louder in my ears. At length, we cleared the forest and stepped out onto the rocks, immersed in the mist that rises from below the falls, what the Makololo call the Mose-ou-Tunga, the Smoke That Thunders. It was at once the most frightening yet marvelous thing I have ever*

experienced, and I count myself the first White man to have ever witnessed it. With a mind to commemorating this, I found a large baobab tree with a hollowed trunk and proceeded to carve my initials therein."

Now, in 1975, Victoria Falls was a popular tourist destination, but to Cecil's knowledge, no one had ever sought out the initials of the famous explorer. There were many islands just above the falls, all of them densely wooded and all but inaccessible. From Livingstone's description, Cecil was certain he could identify the correct island, but could he get there? Most likely, it would involve wading into the wide Zambezi, a potentially deadly undertaking if he should happen to fall and be swept downstream. Even if he could reach the island, would he find the tree still standing and Livingstone's initials still visible inside? He could film them or, better yet, make a plaster cast that he could bring back to England and present to the Royal Geographic Society. His place among the elite members would be secured, perhaps even among modern-day explorers.

A knock on the cabin door disrupted his reverie. Walker, one of his young American charges, stuck his head inside.

"Hey, Cecil, what are you up to?"

"A bit of reading." He pondered closing the book, but decided Walker was worth confiding in. "Actually, I'm reading about David Livingstone's explorations of Victoria Falls. We'll be going there the second week."

"Cool. I've heard they're really awesome."

"Did you know that Livingstone carved his initials in a tree on an island above the falls? To my knowledge, no one's ever found them. Wouldn't it be something to rediscover them?"

"Yeah, I guess so." Walker paused. "Hey, we're getting

pretty bored. There's absolutely nothing to do on this ship."

"Oh, dear. I'll be out in a moment."

"We're back at the pool."

"Yes, yes. Be right out."

Cecil closed the book, returned it to his suitcase, and donned a wide-brimmed hat.

Out on deck, he inhaled the hot, humid air. Such a change from England! The ocean was dead calm, a vast mirror beaming sunlight into his face. They'd been at sea for a week and were likely approaching the equator. Six more days and they'd be in Cape Town.

He approached the stern rail and stared down. The pool was a tiny thing, hardly bigger than a spa. *The Edinburgh Castle* was not one of these new "cruise ships," just a simple transport, and that suited him fine. But the boys were understandably growing bored. Walker and Paul stood in the center of the pool, idly tossing a ball back and forth, while Chas splashed water in Elliott's face. Alec, the oldest boy, had some poor girl pressed against the side. Cecil recognized her as one of a working-class family from Birmingham who was moving to Rhodesia. The father confessed to Cecil that his children were irate about the move, but that there was little economic opportunity for him in England.

"Got a chance to have my own farm in Rhodesia," the man said. "Hire some wogs to work the land."

ABogs, indeed. They might work his farm. Or they might slaughter him and his family in their sleep like the Mau Mau did to the Whites in Kenya. It was a bit late for colonizing.

Spotting Cecil standing at the rail, Paul called out, "Hey, Cecil, why don't you join us? There's room for one more."

Cecil waved back. "No, I'd be burned to a crisp in this sun. In fact, you boys should be getting out. It's just about time for lunch."

Alec continued to nuzzle the girl, her long, dark hair plastered to her chest. She threw occasional glances at the other boys, who stared like a troop of subordinate baboons, waiting for the chance to steal her away from the dominant male.

"Hey, give her a break, man," Paul said.

Alec gave him the finger.

Boys, boys. He loved them at this age, the Americans, anyway. With their golden tans and handsome physiques, they were lovely to look at. And so full of energy. Yes, they could be cynical, but when he got them to Africa, they were invariably filled with wonder. Livingstone saw his mission as bringing Christianity to the Africans; Cecil saw his as bringing boys to Africa.

Knowing how boys loved to test their limits, Cecil gave them as much freedom as he dared on these trips—riding on the roofs of the Land Rovers, stalking game on foot. But now and again, one or another of them went too far. The day before, Paul had been caught climbing the ship's smokestack, quite a feat but strictly prohibited, as signs on the upper deck clearly stated. The captain had been notified and requested a meeting with him and the boys.

Captain MacDonald, a handsome gentleman with a gray mustache and kindly blue eyes, welcomed them into his spacious stateroom. Cecil expected a quick dressing down, but the man seemed in no hurry.

"Please, have a seat," he said. "Tea, anyone?"

"Yes, please," Cecil answered. "A bit of lemon."

The boys declined.

While the steward boiled the water, the captain quizzed Cecil about his group. Where were they from, and what were they about?

"I'm from London," Cecil said. "I take half a dozen boys on an annual safari to South Africa. This group's come all the way from America!"

"That so?" the captain said. "Did you all take a ship from the States?"

"No, we flew to London," Elliott said. "We wish we'd..." His voice trailed off.

The captain smiled. "You wish you'd flown to Cape Town."

"Yes."

Cecil jumped in. "The ship was my idea. I quite enjoy it, actually. Time to relax."

The captain nodded in appreciation, then addressed the boys. "We're a far cry from QE II," he said, referencing the latter of two luxurious ocean liners named after Queen Elizabeth. But you must realize we have certain rules that must be followed for safety's sake. We certainly can't have anyone climbing the stack."

"That was me, sir," Paul said. "I won't do it again."

"And I understand someone has been visiting the First Class lounge, playing the piano?"

Elliot blushed. "Me."

"Yes, we can't have that either. The guests complained to one of the stewards. Something about 'Chopsticks.'"

Chas snickered. "*Chopsticks?*"

"What?" Elliot said. "It's all I know."

The captain smiled again. "We've only got six more days, so let's make the best of it."

"Quite right," Cecil said. "They'll be on their very best

behavior, won't you, boys?"

With that, they were out the door. Cecil was relieved that they'd gotten nothing more than a gentle reprimand.

"Well, that was a lucky break," he said. "No one sent to the brig."

"You sweet-talked him, man," Paul said. "*I brought these boys all the way from America!*"

Cecil had played that card before on these trips. To great effect! South Africans had not seen many Americans since the U.S. Congress introduced that silly law banning trade with their country in opposition to apartheid. The law didn't pass, but it nonetheless dampened South Africa's economy and hurt their pride. These boys would come to see that South Africans were by and large a lovely people. He counted a number of them among his closest friends.

Chapter 3

Olivia Hudson lived in an apartment in Seapoint, Cape Town. Cecil didn't say exactly what their connection was, other than "she's absolutely fabulous" and had graciously invited them all to dinner on their first night. Walker had a vague notion that Olivia, like Cecil, would be a bit of an odd duck. He was surprised to discover upon her opening the door that she was quite beautiful—cornflower blue eyes above high cheekbones, ash-blonde hair pulled back in a short ponytail. She greeted them with a small, lovely smile.

"Come in, please," she said. "Gosh, you American boys are tall."

She ushered them into the living room and asked what she could get them to drink.

"Do you have Coke here?" Elliot asked.

"Of course," she said. "We're not that primitive."

While Olivia went into the kitchen, Walker scanned the framed prints on the wall. There was a Georgia O'Keefe print of a bright white orchid with a pink stamen. He'd seen this one before, heard that it was supposed to allude to female genitalia. Did Olivia like the painting for that reason—the vulva as an object of beauty? The next was an abstract—two dark green rectangles of unequal size pressing in on a thin, blue rectangle. He didn't understand abstract paintings. His art teacher at Choate said you weren't supposed to understand them, that they were there to evoke a feeling. What he felt about this was unease. Why anyone would choose to have it in their house, he didn't understand.

He moved on to the framed photographs. A pair of older adults—Olivia's parents, by the looks of it—beamed at the photographer. And a woman who must be her sister had her arms around two children. There were no shots of Olivia, alone or with anyone else.

Meanwhile, Alec was examining the titles in a floor-to-ceiling bookcase. When Olivia came in with the drinks, he turned to her.

"Have you actually read all these?" he said.

Olivia hesitated. "Yes."

He pulled out a thick book with a weathered binding—*Seven Pillars of Wisdom* by T.E. Lawrence.

"This is Lawrence of Arabia, right? You read this?"

"Yes, he was a fascinating man," Olivia said. "A contradiction in many ways."

"I heard he was a closeted gay," Chas said.

"That's been suggested," she said.

Alec returned the book to the shelf.

"So, how did you boys meet Cecil?" Olivia asked.

Elliot described how Cecil had come to his prep school to show one of his films. Chas and Walker described similar experiences.

"How did *you* meet Cecil?" Schwartzy said to Olivia.

"Oh, everybody knows Cecil," she said. "I can't think

how we first met."

"I was giving a talk on David Livingstone at the Cape Town library," Cecil said. "Surely, you remember that. You came up afterwards and told me about your work promoting women's health amongst the Africans."

"Yes, I think you said I was wasting my time."

Cecil frowned. "I don't know about that."

She turned back to Schwartzy. "He's visited me every year since. Always brings a new crop of handsome boys. When are you going to bring some girls along, Cecil?"

"That wouldn't work," he said. "There's no privacy on these trips." He added with a chuckle, "We all sleep and shit in the bush."

As he listened to the back and forth, Walker decided there was no sexual relationship between Cecil and Olivia. Cecil had mentioned he was sixty years old and never married. The man was probably gay, though he was wise not to admit it if that were true. No parent would allow their teenaged son on a trip with an avowed homosexual. What about Olivia? She was beautiful, in her thirties, a catch for any man, but apparently single. Was she a lesbian? Walker had never met one, so he couldn't say for sure.

Olivia caught him staring. "Walker, what do you make of South Africa so far?"

"It's beautiful," he said. "But this apartheid thing is pretty weird."

"Oh? What have you witnessed?"

He told her how he and Schwartzy had stood in the Non-Whites line at the post office as a show of solidarity but had been shooed away by the Africans themselves.

Olivia laughed. "No, you can't do that kind of thing here. You'd be putting *their* lives in jeopardy."

"That's what we figured."

Schwartzy jumped in. "What do *you* think about apartheid?"

Her face took on a serious expression. "It's a terrible policy. We've got to give the Blacks equal standing, but I don't think it can happen right away."

"Why not?"

"We're outnumbered five to one. You can imagine what might happen."

The room fell silent. Walker pictured it—people being slaughtered in the streets, in their homes. No matter what your sympathies, you could find yourself caught in the middle. These people were trapped. Olivia was trapped.

The timer went off in the kitchen. Olivia retrieved a pot roast from the oven and set it on the counter, its wonderful aroma filling the small apartment. She instructed everyone to serve themselves. They dished their plates and returned to their seats.

"So, where do we go for some fun in this town?" Chas said.

"Do you mean tonight?" Olivia said. "I don't know, really. I don't go out much."

"Seriously?"

"I mostly hang out with a few close friends over a bottle of wine."

Walker wondered at that remark. If Olivia were truly gay, she might not be in the habit of going out at night, not in this country. That thought made him deeply sad.

"In any case, we're not going to be having a late night of it," Cecil said. "Olivia's got something planned for you tomorrow."

She brightened. "Yes, I've suggested that while Cecil

does his grocery shopping, you boys hike up Table Mountain. I've got a friend who'll lead you. Would you like that? Get a little exercise?"

A chorus of "yeahs" circled the table.

"Fabulous," she said. "He'll meet you in the morning. His name's Thomas."

When the time came to say goodbye, Walker made a point of thanking Olivia for dinner and for arranging the hike. "It's very kind of you," he said.

A strand of hair had fallen across her face. She brushed it away and took his hand.

"It was nice to meet you, too," she said. "I hope you'll come back."

She didn't mean it in the way he wished, but it sent him out the door in a dream.

That night, as he lay in bed at the guesthouse, he reflected on the day. The past year had been deeply unsettling for him. Somewhere between his reading of existential philosophy and conversation with friends, he'd lost his belief in God. He'd begun to doubt there was even such a thing as freedom of choice, that perhaps he was just a robot adrift in a meaningless universe. He'd felt a lack of purpose and had only dark thoughts about the future. But since he'd stepped off the boat that morning, he'd felt the curtain lifting.

He reached into his duffle bag and took out the one book that hadn't been taken from him—*The Essays of Henry D. Thoreau*. He read the table of contents and turned to the essay entitled "Walking."

"I wish to speak a word for Nature," Thoreau wrote, *"for absolute freedom and wildness, as contrasted with a freedom and culture merely civil. If you are ready to leave father and mother,*

brother and sister, and wife and child and friends...if you have paid your debts, and made your will, and settled all your affairs, and are a free man...then you are ready for a walk."

Thomas arrived in the morning, tricked out in shorts and hiking boots. Save for his accent, he could have passed for an American. He matched Alec's height, his light brown hair cut short. Walker had yet to see any South African male with shoulder-length hair like his, an attribute no doubt associated with a hippie lifestyle not yet accepted in this country. Either way, Thomas appeared not to mind, welcoming the boys with a ready smile, eager to show them Cape Town's natural wonders.

They parked at the base of Table Mountain, its 3,500-foot-tall, two-mile-wide face filling the horizon. A dark pine forest at the base transitioned to steep, brush-covered slopes and ended in sheer, broken cliffs. Walker was disappointed to see a cable car running to the top—an engineering marvel that tamed a summit otherwise reachable only by the strong. But as soon as he set foot on the dirt path, his leg muscles and lungs put to the task, he forgot about the tram.

The route they took followed the Platteklip Gorge straight up the mountain. Ascending beyond the pine forest, they entered a magical landscape of boulders and shrubs interspersed with purple, yellow, and red wildflowers.

Thomas motioned at the ground. "This is called fynbos," he said. "It's a suite of plants only found in the Southern Cape, nowhere else in the world."

He lifted a branch. "Feel how waxy these leaves are.

They've evolved to survive in this harsh environment."

Walker put on his 50mm lens and focused in on one of the leaves. Schwartzy, meanwhile, had managed to scale one of the boulders. He put on a telephoto lens and aimed it at the city below.

"Good shot?" Walker called.

"Yeah, man. It's like a Picasso."

He imagined what Schwartzy was seeing through that lens—a hazy tapestry of blocks, cross-hatched by lines. Walker was a literal photographer, while Schwartzy was a true artist. He could learn to see from his friend but would always be a step behind.

Thomas made his way over to a west-facing ledge. "Guys, come over here," he said. "There's a great view of the Lion's Head."

Walker picked his way through the shrubs to the edge of the cliff. Below him, Table Mountain dropped a thousand feet, tapering down to a narrow ridge and rising again as a pyramid-shaped peak that did, indeed, look like a lion's head. Beyond the head, spreading to the horizon, lay the shimmering Atlantic Ocean.

"You're actually seeing two oceans," Thomas said. "The Indian and the Atlantic."

Walker stared. "That's where they meet?"

"More or less."

He felt dizzy, ecstatic. He'd read somewhere about "power spots," places on earth where you could feel the power of the universe, where supernatural things were possible. This felt like one of them.

"Let's keep going," Thomas said. "We've got a steep climb ahead."

Further up the mountain, Thomas paused to point out

what looked like a brown goat perched on an outcropping. "There's your first African wildlife," he said. "Only it's not native. It's a Himalayan tahr. Back in the 1930s, a pair of them escaped from the Cape Town zoo. They found the land to their liking and have thrived ever since."

"Kind of like the Whites," Schwartzy said.

Thomas blanched. Walker scoffed. "Jesus, Schwartzy. Leave it alone."

The final hundred yards was a near-vertical pitch. Walker leaned forward, hands to the ground, and crawled to the top, panting for breath. He turned to take in the view—cape, city, ocean, sky. He felt like he was flying.

"There's a restroom just over there if anyone needs it," Thomas said.

Walker came back to Earth. He did, in fact, need to piss. He approached the restroom, a handsome structure built of rough-hewn stone. Whoever designed it had made sure it blended in with the mountain. A brass sign hung over the entrance.

Net Blankes, it read. *Whites Only.*

Chapter 4

Loading day. Cecil instructed the boys to put their duffle bags in the back of the blue Land Rover. His Rover, the red one, was already packed with wooden crates containing the stove, cookware, canned food, and cots. On the roof of both cars, a rack held metal jerry cans filled with gasoline and plastic cans filled with drinking water.

When everything was packed, Cecil unfolded a map of South Africa on the hood of his car and directed the boys to gather around.

"We'll be driving up Highway 7 through the west side of the country," he said. "This should be a good road paved all the way. We'll spend the night with some friends of mine just outside of Vredendal."

He pointed to a small dot on the map, some fifty miles inland from the Atlantic coast.

"Do they have beds for all of us?" Elliot wanted to know.

"We'll be sleeping in our own cots, probably out in their garage. They're making us dinner, which is quite enough to ask."

Walker asked if they would see any wildlife. Cecil explained that they would mostly be driving through farm country, the only wildlife likely to be the occasional scrub hare flattened on the road. Walker nodded. Despite what television shows portrayed, he understood that Africa was not all lions and wildebeest striding across the Serengeti.

"We'll ride three people per car," Cecil said. "Doesn't matter who goes with whom. Paul, why don't you and Chas ride with me today? Walker and Elliot go with Alec."

Alec was not Walker's preferred company, but there were many days of driving to come.

"Mind if I ride shotgun?" he said to Elliot.

Elliot shrugged. "Go ahead."

Walker settled into the front passenger seat—on the left-hand side—and closed the door with a metallic clang. He'd ridden in one of these Land Rovers back home and recognized the spartan interior—vinyl seats, a four-speed stick shift, a speedometer that topped out at 75 mph, no air-conditioning, no radio.

Alec got behind the wheel and set a small canvas bag on the floor between them. He turned the key and pushed the starter. The 67-horsepower engine came to life. Feeble as they sounded, these engines reportedly lasted forever and, in four-wheel drive, should get them through the roughest roads.

Alec pulled out behind Cecil and deftly double-clutched between first and second gear. They drove through the city and onto a four-lane highway.

"Looks like you've got the shifting down," Walker said.

Alec stared. "I know how to do it."

"I thought you had trouble earlier."

"Nope."

"Then, what took you so long to get back to the guest house?"

"I made a little stop along the way."

Alec nodded at the bag on the floor. "Open it up. Check it out."

Walker unzipped the bag, reached inside, and felt the hard contours of a pistol. He lifted up what looked like an old West six-shooter.

"It's a Ruger Blackhawk," Alec said. "Three-fifty-seven Magnum."

"You bought this?" Walker said. "I thought you had to be, like, twenty-one to buy a pistol."

"Not here."

Walker turned the gun over in his hand. "You'll never get this back through customs."

"Maybe not. At least I'll have some protection while I'm here."

"From what? A lion?"

"A lion. Some crazy African."

Walker felt the blood rise to his head. They hadn't been in the country two days, and Alec was thinking about shooting Africans instead of befriending them.

Elliot leaned forward from the back seat. "Can I see it?"

"No, put it back," Alec said. "And don't tell Cecil about this. Either of you."

"We won't," Elliot said. "My Dad has a Ruger. A rifle."

"Oh, yeah? What model?"

"I don't know. He bought it to go on a hunting safari in Kenya."

"It's probably a three-seventy-five. What did he shoot?"

"All kinds of stuff. An impala. A zebra. A hippopotamus."

"He shot a hippo?" Walker said. "Why?"

"I'm not sure. He had the impala head mounted and the zebra skin made into a rug, but for the hippo, he just kept the feet. They made them into wastebaskets."

Walker scoffed. "Your dad shot a hippo so he could have its feet made into wastebaskets?"

"No! I think he just wanted to shoot it."

Walker shook his head. Trophy hunting seemed cool back in his youth. Some of his friends' dads had an antlered buck or two hanging on their living room wall, but a hippopotamus? To be turned into wastebaskets?

He cranked down the window and let the cool, dry air waft across his face. Outside, tract houses gave way to flat agricultural fields. The landscape bore a strong resemblance to the American West, giant center-pivot irrigation systems circling fields of alfalfa, wheat, and corn. Mountains in the distance. Blue sky overhead.

The miles rolled by to the whine of the heavily treaded tires.

"So, where are you going to go to college?" he said to Alec.

"Who said I was going to college?"

"You graduated, right?"

"Yup."

"Did you apply to college?"

"Yup."

Walker waited. "Did you get accepted anywhere?"

"Williams. Trinity. I haven't decided if I'm going to go. I might take some time off."

This surprised Walker. People talked about taking a year off before college, but he didn't know anyone who'd actually done that. Alec must have more confidence than most. Than him, anyway.

"What do your parents want you to do?" he asked.

"My *parent* wants me to go to Williams, but it's not up to her."

Another surprise. In Walker's world, almost everyone was from a two-parent household. Were Alec's parents divorced? Had his father died?

"So, what are you going to do when you get back from Africa?"

"Haven't really thought about it."

Haven't thought about it. Right.

Up ahead, Cecil's Land Rover slowed in front of a split-level ranch house. A station wagon stood in the paved driveway, a flower garden in the yard, a cultivated field out back. This was not the Africa Walker was hoping for.

The Appletons were a pleasant couple, friends of Cecil's from England who'd moved to South Africa some years before. They welcomed the boys into their thoroughly modern home and apologized for not having enough bedrooms.

"Hope you boys don't mind sleeping in the garage," Mr. Appleton said. "I've cleaned it up."

They occupied the sofas and chairs in the living room and named their preference in sodas.

"And how are you liking our country so far?" Mr. Appleton said to the group.

"It's beautiful!" Elliot said. "Yesterday, we hiked up Table Mountain."

"Marvelous view from up there."

Walker stared through the picture window at the planted field behind the house.

"How big is your farm?" he asked.

"It's a bit over three thousand acres," Mr. Appleton said.

"Wow, that's huge!"

"About average for this part of the country."

Schwartzy glanced around the room, taking in the

framed prints of what looked to be European mountain scenery.

"Cecil said you're from England," he said. "What made you move down here?"

"Oh, goodness, we couldn't have all this in England," Mrs. Appleton said. "The land would cost a fortune if you could even find it."

"No, you couldn't," Mr. Appleton said. "We couldn't."

"Think you'll have it for long?" Schwartzy said with a smile.

Mrs. Appleton blanched. "What do you mean?"

"I mean, what if the Africans want it back? You know, the land and everything."

Cecil clucked. "Good lord, Paul. What a thing to say!"

"I'm just asking."

Mrs. Appleton sighed. "I certainly hope it won't come to that."

"You know, we're quite liberal here in the Cape Province," Mr. Appleton said. "We actually allowed Blacks and Coloreds to vote back in the day. The Afrikaners put an end to that."

He went on to explain that the White Afrikaners dominated the government of South Africa. He spoke of their recent creation of Bantustans, nominally independent states where all Blacks were now required to live, deprived of all political and civil rights as South Africans.

"A bit like your Indian reservations," he said. "Crowded together on the poorest land. Stuck out in the middle of nowhere."

"Why not make Blacks citizens of South Africa?" Walker said. "It's worked out for us. Mostly."

Mr. Appleton shook his head. "I'm afraid our Blacks are not like yours."

Schwartzy rolled his eyes.

"He's right, you know," Cecil said. "The Africans have made a mess of every country they've taken charge of."

Cecil's comment made Walker angry. He was aware of the reported corruption and mismanagement in many Black African-ruled countries, but maybe things could be different in South Africa. Then again, he didn't live here, didn't have anything to lose. The Appletons and people like them had everything to lose.

He decided to change the subject. "When might we see some wildlife?"

Mr. Appleton brightened. "You're headed up to South West tomorrow? I expect you'll see some springbok. The odd aardwolf, a bit like a hyena."

"An aardwolf! I'd like to see one of those."

Walker was glad to have the conversation turn back towards nature. This was something everyone valued, everyone loved. He carried that thought with him to dinner and on into the night.

Chapter 5

After breakfast, they got back in the Rovers, Walker and Schwartzy riding with Cecil in the red car. They left behind the cultivated fields and entered a landscape of red clay hills with a sparse cover of yellow grass. Cecil was in an upbeat mood, excited about entering "the bush."

As they crested a hill, Cecil pointed to the right. "There's a springbok. Do you see him?"

Walker scanned the grassland and spotted the antelope standing about a hundred feet off the road. It was the size and shape of an American pronghorn antelope with golden tan flanks, a white belly, and short black horns. Upon seeing the Land Rover, it broke into a run. Walker assumed it would run away from the car, but instead it ran parallel, matching their 55-mph speed. Suddenly, it crossed the road just ahead of them and began bouncing in the air on rigid legs as if they were made of springs.

"What the hell is he doing?" Schwartzy said.

"It's called pronking," Cecil said. "They do that to throw predators off. He thinks we're a cheetah!"

Walker imagined running behind the springbok, trying to predict where it would go next. Impossible! He turned in his seat to watch the animal disappear over a ridge.

"If you'd gotten a film of that, you could have put it on *National Geographic!*" he said.

Cecil laughed. "I don't know about that. They're quite common, actually."

Walker got out his camera and screwed on the 300mm telephoto lens. In a matter of minutes, they came upon a group of four springbok standing at a distance.

"There's some more!" he said. "Can we stop?"

Cecil slowed and pulled to the side of the road, waving for Alec to pull in behind him. Walker had just aimed his camera out the window when the blue Rover flew past.

"God damnit!" Cecil said. "I told him to stay behind me."

The Land Rover sped on into the distance.

"I'm sorry, but we can't stop," Cecil said. He pulled back on the road, caught up to Alec and began flashing his lights. Alec slowed. Cecil came abreast and yelled out the window.

"What the hell do you think you're doing?"

Alec shrugged.

"You're never to pass me, do you understand? You have no idea where we're going."

In mid-afternoon, they reached the Orange River, the boundary between South Africa and South West Africa. Crossing the bridge at Vioolsdriff, Walker stared down at a shallow watercourse as wide as a football field, brown, not orange. On the South West African side, a thin band of irrigated fields bordered the floodplain, beyond which desert sands and treeless mountains rose to the cloudless sky.

The road followed the river for a time, the fields disappearing as the river entered a shallow canyon. Cecil slowed. Just ahead, a dry wash wound in from the right, bordered by a sandy jeep track.

"There's a lovely campsite just up here," he said. "The Appletons told me about this."

Cecil put the Land Rover into four-wheel drive and turned onto the track. Walker's heart quickened as they wound among the rocky hills. There could definitely be wildlife here.

A quarter-mile in, Cecil came to a halt. There was no sign to identify this as a campsite, but a fire ring beside the creek bed showed it had been used as such.

"This is it!" Cecil said. Walker stepped out and surveyed the surroundings. A low, scalable cliff on the far side of the creek offered the possibility of sneaking up on any animals that lay beyond. And the creek bed itself, a sandy surface perfect for showing animal tracks, would be worth exploring.

"Alright, get your cots out and set them up however you wish," Cecil said. "This isn't lion country, so you needn't be close together."

This was their first night camping out, and Walker felt like getting a little distance from the others. He chose a spot close to the creek, while the others clustered around the cars. Cecil took out the gas cookstove and set it up by the fire ring.

"Someone bring me a can of water," he said.

Schwartzy did his monkey thing, springing onto the hood of the red Land Rover and wrestling a jerry can down from the roof rack.

Once the campsite was set up, Cecil suggested a walk.

"Get what you need out of the cars and then close them up," he said.

"Shall I bring my camera?" Elliot said.

"I shouldn't think we'd see any game, but you never know."

"Okay, I'll leave it."

Walker vowed never to be unprepared and so grabbed his out of the car. They'd walked a hundred feet along the creek bed when Elliot changed his mind.

"I think I'll go back and get mine," he said.

Walker and Schwartzy traded looks. This kid could decide nothing for himself.

As the group waited for Elliot to return, Walker pointed to a set of tracks in the sand.

"Cecil, look at these. What do you think made them?"

"Some kind of antelope, I would guess. Possibly a kudu."

Walker stared down the length of the creek bed. It was impossible to tell how long ago the tracks had been made, but he held out hope that they were recent. The sandy surface silenced their footsteps, and maybe, just maybe, they would sneak up on the animal from behind. He scanned the ledge. This would be a good place for a klipspringer, a tiny antelope that favored rocky environs. But after half an hour of walking, they'd seen nothing.

"Alright, let's head back," Cecil said. "It's getting on towards sundown."

As they approached the camp, a loud bark rang out. Atop the ledge stood an animal with a nose like a dog and a heavy brow of a Neanderthal man. A baboon! Others sprang from the campground, leaving behind a trail of garbage.

"Oh, Christ," Cecil said. "Who left the car door open?"

It was the blue Land Rover, the one that Elliot had been riding in, the one that held his camera.

"I thought I closed it," he said.

"You idiot!" Cecil said. "Thank God they didn't get into the car with the food."

The baboons had gotten into the boys' duffle bags, scattering their belongings across the ground. Schwartzy picked up a tube of toothpaste. "Look, they gnawed right through this thing! I can't believe it!"

Cecil smirked. "Yes, our baboons are not like yours."

Cecil opened the back of the red Land Rover and got out the wooden crates with the food and cookware. He set up the gas cookstove by the fire ring and chose two cans of pork and beans.

"Open these, if you would," he said to Walker.

Walker hunted for the can opener and set to work unscrewing the tops.

"Good lad," Cecil said. "I see you've done this before."

"Yeah, I went to canoe camp. All we ate was canned food."

When dinner was warmed, Cecil called the other boys over. He dished out the pork and beans and passed around a bottle of ketchup, what Cecil referred to as "tomato sauce."

"This is actually pretty good," Schwartzy said.

"Best thing I've had out of a can," Chas added.

Walker gazed at the cliff, now in silhouette against the yellowing sky. He pictured the baboons sneaking up to the edge, raising their snouts to the delicious smells. They'd freaked him out, but now the lesson was learned. Nothing would be left open. They weren't in Connecticut anymore.

That evening, he took out his Thoreau and read by flashlight.

The West of which I speak is but another name for the Wild, and what I have been preparing to say is that in Wildness is the preserva-

tion of the World...Our ancestors were savages. The story of Romulus and Remus being suckled by the wolf is not a meaningless fable. The founders of every state which has risen to eminence have drawn their nourishment and vigor from a similar source...I believe in the forest, and in the meadow, and in the night in which the corn grows.

※

Walker woke up in the middle of the night, freezing cold. No one had told him it could be like this in Africa. He glanced around the campground and saw that Elliot's cot was empty. Had he moved into one of the Rovers to stay warm? He got up and shined his flashlight though the cars' windows—no one there. He aimed the beam down the jeep track they'd come in on, and there was Elliot, standing in his T-shirt and underpants. Walker approached him from behind.

"Elliot, what are you doing?"

Elliot turned. "Is this the driveway to the Chockley's house?"

"The Chockleys?"

"They're friends of my parents."

"What are you talking about?"

Walker realized then that Elliot was sleepwalking. He'd heard about this phenomenon but never actually witnessed it. "We're in Africa, Elliot," he said. "Come on, I'll take you back to your cot."

Elliot followed, climbed into his sleeping bag, and closed his eyes as if nothing had happened.

The next morning, Walker woke to the soothing song of the ring-necked dove—*kuk-COOOR-uk, kuk-COOOR-uk*. Cecil was up preparing breakfast.

"Tea for you?" Cecil said. "I've got the water boiling."

Walker wiped his eyes and eased out of his sleeping bag. "I've never actually had tea. What kind is it?"

"English breakfast tea. The only kind I drink."

Cecil handed him a steaming tin cup. Walker took a sip, the bitter taste causing him to gag.

"Ooof. Do we have any sugar?"

"You Americans. Always have to sweeten things up."

Walker glanced at the others, still tucked in their bags. "Elliot was sleepwalking last night," he said to Cecil. "I found him standing in the road, asking if that was the way to some friend of his parents' house."

"Was he? He didn't mention anything about that in his application."

Cecil studied the sleeping boy. "I shan't worry about it unless he does it again. Let's keep an eye on him."

Cecil threw a quarter stick of butter in a small pot. When that was melted, he cracked open a few eggs and stirred them together. An equal amount of butter went into a frying pan along with a slice of bread. Once the bread was browned, he forked it onto a tin plate and ladled the scrambled eggs on top.

"Chop, chop, everyone," he said. "Breakfast is ready!"

Walker took the first plate and bit into the soft, buttery toast with its topping of eggs. "This is pretty good!" he said.

Cecil smiled. "Eggs Covington," he said. "I knew you'd like it!"

All during breakfast, Walker kept an eye on Elliot, trying to determine if the boy remembered the events of the past night. He gave no indication of that, wolfing down his eggs without looking up. Walker felt he needed to bring it up, but not in front of the others. When Elliot got up to use the "bush toilet," Walker saw his chance.

"I'll take the shovel and toilet paper when you're done," he said.

Elliot nodded and ventured off into the woods. Walker was waiting when the boy came out.

"Hey, do you know you were sleepwalking last night?" he said.

"I was?"

"Yes, I found you standing in the road. You asked if that was the driveway to somebody named the Chockleys."

Elliot furrowed his brow. "Oh, yeah. I dreamed I was trying to find their house."

"Do you do this a lot?"

"Only when we travel, I think."

"Well, you need to be careful out here."

Elliot nodded. "Don't tell the others. They'll make fun of me."

"I already told Cecil, but I won't speak to anyone else."

"Okay, thanks."

Back at camp, the boys washed their dishes in two rubber containers—one with hot, soapy water, the other clear rinse water. When that was done, they loaded all the gear into the Rovers. Cecil took out a map and outlined their route for the day.

"We're driving north about hundred and fifty kilometers to a town called Luderitz. Lovely little seaside village. We'll have lunch there, then go in search of a colony of fur seals. They're sea lions, actually. I don't know exactly where they are, but I'll ask around. It should be a real adventure!"

Walker smiled at the thought of seeing some exotic wildlife. Instructed by Cecil to join him and Chas in the red Rover, he asked if he could ride on the roof.

"I should think so," Cecil said. "It's a good road. Won't be much traffic. Bang on the roof if you want me to stop. We might see some more antelope along the way, maybe an ostrich."

"Cool. Chas, do you want to join me up top?"

Chas shook his head. "I prefer the luxury of vinyl seats."

"You sure?"

"Go for it, big boy."

With that, Walker climbed the metal rungs on the back of the car and hoisted himself onto the plywood platform. The jerry cans set into the roof rack just above the windshield offered a perfect handhold. He banged on the roof to let Cecil know he was ready.

Cecil turned the ignition and started down the jeep track, the car swaying from side to side as it rolled across the uneven ground. Walker gripped the handles. This was going to take some getting used to. They reached the paved highway and turned north. As the Rover came up to speed, the wind blew back his hair. The smell of dry grass filled his nostrils, the sun warmed his face. This was joy! This was freedom! This was Africa!

Over the course of the morning, the greenery that bordered the Orange River gave way to a moonscape of red sand and rock. The miles rolled by without revealing a house or even a passing car. Walker appreciated the stark beauty to the terrain, but within an hour's time, he'd had enough. His eyes were dried out and itching. He banged on the roof. The slowed to a halt, and he hopped back inside.

"Have fun up there?" Chas asked.

"It's pretty cool. A little tough on the eyes," Walker said. "You should try it."

"Not my high."

Another hour passed before they reached the first sign of civilization. The crossroads town of Aus consisted of a train station, a hotel, a few shops, and a garage. A church steeple rose above a bedraggled cluster of trees.

"Why would anyone want to live here?" Chas said.

"It's a stop on the railway line from Keetmanshoop to Luderitz," Cecil said. "In World War One, it was a prisoner-of-war camp for German soldiers."

"Of course," Chas said. "Where are you going to run to?"

At the lone intersection, Cecil turned east, and they entered once again into the land of sand and rock. Much as Walker wanted to take in all of Africa, he couldn't stay awake. He leaned against the window and closed his eyes.

Cecil's voice woke him from his sleep. "Here we are, boys."

The tractless desert had been transformed into another world. Tudor-style houses with red tile roofs spread across rocky hillside. A neo-Gothic church rose into the cloudless sky. And beyond the church lay the misty blue Atlantic Ocean.

Chas read out the street signs. "Wagenbauer, Bismarck, Vogelsang...Did the German prisoners escape to here?"

"This was a German colony before the war, don't you know that?" Cecil said.

"Missed that in my tenth-grade European Colonialism course."

Walker laughed but had to admit he hadn't known

that either. Compared to the English, Americans seemed relatively ignorant of world history. This was reinforced when they pulled in front of a restaurant—The Portuguese Fisherman.

"Let me guess," Chas said. "The Portuguese were here before the Germans."

"That's right," Cecil said. "The Portuguese arrived in the 1400s. The Germans came in the 1800s. The English... Oh, never mind. You wouldn't be interested."

They passed through the front door into a sea of white—white walls, white tables, white chairs. A waitress pulled two tables together. She poured each of them a glass of water, Walker finishing his in two long gulps. She handed out the menus, the boys each ordering a hamburger.

"No one's going to order seafood?" Cecil said. "Good God, I should have left you all at home."

After lunch, Cecil queried the Portuguese manager about the sea lion colony. Yes, they'd recently been seen along the coast, a dozen miles to the south.

"Not much of a road there," the man said. "Mind you don't get lost."

The group headed back to the parking lot, Walker resuming his perch atop the red Land Rover. Cecil drove through the town to what was little more than a sand track bordering the ocean, no sign giving the road a name or suggesting where it went. Cecil put the Rover in four-wheel drive and eased into the sand.

Despite his high vantage point, Walker could see nothing of the actual coast. A thick mist hung over the water, and a steep cliff blocked his view of the beach. A few miles in, he heard a sound like barking dogs. Lots of them. He tapped on the roof. Cecil stopped.

"Do you hear that?" Walker called.

Cecil shut off the engine. The barking was nearer now. "That's it!" he said.

Cecil put the Land Rover back in gear and drove to a point just above the cacophony of sound. As the car came to a halt, Walker scrambled off the roof and ran to the edge of the cliff. He couldn't see the animals through the mist, but the chorus of barking and the smell of shit belied their presence.

A steep, sandy slope led to the beach. The boys started down. Cecil called for them to wait.

"I must get my camera," he said.

Walker stewed as Cecil opened the back of the car and fumbled with the boxes. Jesus. Did the man always have to store the camera away? And bring a tripod?

"Fuck it, I'm going down," Schwartzy said.

Walker waited until Cecil arrived, then half-slid, half-ran down the cliff.

"Be careful!" Cecil called after him. "Sea lions can be rather large!"

Walker reached solid ground, where he joined Schwartzy and started down the beach. The thick mist all but blotted out the sun and cut the ground visibility to dozens of yards. This was going to test the limits of their Kodachrome 25 film.

"What shutter speed are you using?" he asked.

"I'm going with one-thirtieth."

"Shit, that's slow."

"Best we can do."

Alec, marching ahead of them, came to a halt. A dark brown form seven feet long rose up from the sand. Alec yelled, "Wooh! Wooh!" and the sea lion started flopping on fins toward the ocean. Here rose another and another. The entire beach was transformed into a sea of moving bodies. Walker raised his camera and shot. He wound the film lever, moved forward, and shot again. This was D-Day with a camera!

At one point, Walker found himself between a big bull and the water. The animal came toward him at the speed of a runner, white teeth flashing from his open mouth. Walker waved his arms. The animal veered away, flopped past, and disappeared into the surf.

In minutes, it was over. The entire colony was in the water, heads bobbing above the waves. The boys stood panting, laughing.

"I almost touched one of them!" Schwartzy said.

"Me, too!" Elliot gushed.

Cecil arrived clutching his movie camera and tripod. "That was fantastic!" he said. "I filmed you all running right amongst them!"

"Man, I can't wait to see that!" Walker said.

Years later, he would cringe at that scene in Cecil's movie. People came to consider it cruel to chase a colony of sea lions into the ocean. That would get them thrown out of any national park. But on this day, in this place, he felt like the luckiest boy on the planet. And Cecil was his hero.

⊗

From Luderitz, they headed back east, bound for a mountain range—the Nauklufts—that Cecil claimed harbored an uncommon species of zebra. He hoped to film them, of course, adding to his documentation of the unusual.

"What do you plan to do with this year's film, other

than show it at schools?" Walker said.

"I should hope to sell it to *National Geographic*."

"Have you ever sold one to them before?"

"Yes, I sold them a film on elephants some years ago."

"Was it ever shown on TV?"

Cecil frowned. "I don't believe so. They've gotten quite picky."

Chas rolled his eyes.

Back at Aus, they turned north, rising over low mountains, down to the desert, and up again. Late in the afternoon, they skirted a spectacular array of red sand dunes that rose like a petrified sea to the east. Walker asked if they could stop somewhere to photograph them. Cecil found a side road that led right to the base of the dunes.

Walker stepped out and started to photograph the nearest dune—a sprawling serpent at least three hundred feet tall. Without asking permission, Alec started to climb it.

"Don't take long," Cecil called. "We've got a lot of distance yet to cover."

As Alec plodded up the ridge, Walker focused in on him—the perfect image of a man alone in the world—and snapped away with his camera.

Elliot, meanwhile, wandered along the base of the dune. "Hey, guys! Look what I found!" He pointed to a giant green beetle rolling an earthen ball four times its size up the side of the dune.

"That's a dung beetle," Cecil said. "They form animal shit into a ball and roll it to their nests to eat."

Walker stared at the insect, struggling to roll the ball up the endless slope. "Where's he going with it?" he said. "There's nothing up there but sand."

"He's probably trying to get to the other side," Elliot

said. "We should carry him over there."

"And deprive him of the meaning of his life?" Chas said. "Leave him alone."

"We *should* help him," Walker said. "He doesn't realize what he's doing is pointless."

"Oh, really?' Chas said. "What are you doing that's so meaningful?"

Walker froze. The comment hit him unexpectedly hard. He turned away, his eyes burning.

Alec returned from his conquest of the dune. "Okay, I'm ready to go," he said.

Back on the road, the low sun turned the landscape a brilliant orange, like a scene from a movie depicting the end of the world. While Walker stewed, Chas dozed in the backseat. How could he be so smart and not be interested in what lay all around them? Maybe he understood the big picture in life and didn't need to be bothered with the details.

Cecil glanced over. "I heard what Chas said to you. Don't pay any attention to him. You've got a lot going on in your life."

"I don't know. He's pretty smart."

Cecil put his hand on his knee. "Don't be silly."

They rode on through the desert, the sun dropping below the horizon.

"When are we going to get there?" Walker said.

"Shouldn't be much farther," Cecil replied.

They reached a side road that headed into the Naulkuft Mountains, now a jagged silhouette against the purple sky. The Rover rocked from side to side as it crawled up the canyon, crossed a stream—a stream!—and came to the road's end.

"Here we are," Cecil said.

Walker stepped out, the silence reverberating in his ears. A single fire ring stood beneath a grove of thorn trees. From somewhere beyond came the faint trickle of moving water.

The other car arrived. Schwartzy, Elliot, and Alec emerged looking like zombies.

Alec stared around. "Why did we come here, again?"

"I'm hoping to see Hartmann's mountain zebra," Cecil said. "It's a subspecies you only find here in the Nauklufts."

"When are we going to see some lions?"

"This isn't lion country," Cecil said. "We may see some in the Etosha Pan. Just be patient."

Alec picked up a rock and chucked it against a tree. It hit with a resounding *thock*.

Daybreak in the bush. Here it was again—the call of the African dove. Walker rolled over to locate the birds and saw one in the thorn tree and another picking at seeds on the dusty ground. The morning sun lit up the brushy mountainside. Another cloudless day.

Walker recalled Alec's protest the night before. He, for one, was glad to be here. The prospect of hiking through the hills, searching for wildlife was the reason he'd come here. So what if it was only for zebras? When was the last time any of them had seen such an animal in the wild?

He pulled on his pants, shoes, and shirt and surveyed the surroundings. The others still dozed, sleeping bags pulled tight around their necks. Just as well. He could take a walk by himself. The stream would be a good place to start. He grabbed his camera and followed a path through the thorn trees.

Entering the clearing, he slowed his steps. If there was any wildlife around, it would likely be here. As expected, the stream was small. A flock of small olive-colored birds gathered at the water's edge. Alarmed by his presence, they flew into the thorn trees across the stream, where they perched in the open, golden jewels in the morning light. He took a few photographs, then proceeded on downstream.

Here was something else—what looked like a giant scrotum hanging from a tree branch. A yellow, robin-sized bird emerged from a hole in the bottom. This must be its nest! He took a few more photos and hurried back to camp.

Cecil was up, preparing breakfast.

"Cecil, I found a bird nest about two feet long!"

"That's a weaver bird," Cecil said. "They build nests much larger than that. Some as big as haystacks. You'll see."

Not for the first time, his leader threw cold water on one of his discoveries. Yes, the nest, the bird, the animal might be commonplace to an African veteran, but why not share in the excitement of a newcomer to the continent?

"Get the others up, will you?" Cecil said. "I'm anxious to look for those zebra."

Walker shook off his disappointment and roused the others from their sleep. They got up and peed, picked up their mess kits, and stood in line.

"We'll be hiking today," Cecil said. "No more driving."

"Thank God," Chas said. "My ass is getting beat to a pulp."

The trailhead left out from the campground, following

the now-dry stream. Here beside the trail was an enormous plant that looked like a collapsed palmetto, broad green leaves radiating out from a central stem and lying in a heap on the ground.

"That's a welwitschia plant," Cecil said. "Quite odd, isn't it?"

"Is it dead?" Walker asked.

"No, that's just how they look. Some sort of accommodation to the heat," Cecil said. "Some of them live to be a thousand years old."

Walker took several shots of this, including a closeup of the cluster of red seeds that rose from the middle of the plant. Trailing just behind, Elliot took the exact same shots. Chas whispered in Walker's ear, "Tell him to come up with his own shots," but Walker decided to leave him alone. Why spoil this experience for anyone?

For the first mile or two, they saw nothing other than small birds. Then, Schwartzy called out, "Zebras!"

Across a low valley, partially hidden behind the thorn bushes, stood a line of zebras. They had spotted the hikers and had their ears up, listening.

"Those are Hartmann's!" Cecil cried. "Do you see how the stripes go all the way around? Plains zebras have a perfectly white belly."

It seemed like a minor difference, but if it was remarkable to Cecil, then it was worth noting. Walker clicked away with his still camera while Cecil's Bolex whirred beside him.

"Did you get the stallion?" Schwartzy asked. "He has kind of a dewlap."

"I got him," Walker said.

As if having overheard the conversation, the stallion broke into a trot, with the rest of the herd following behind. It was a beautiful sight—the black-and-white striped animals moving across a tapestry of maroon and yellow. In moments, they were gone over the ridge.

"That was simply wonderful," Cecil said. "You boys were lucky to see this."

They retreated back to camp for lunch. With the sun straight overhead, Africa seemed to take a nap. Birds fell silent. Animals were nowhere to be seen. The boys turned to their books, all except Elliot, who sat chewing his fingernails.

Chas brushed a lock of red hair from his forehead. "Do you mind?"

Elliot paused. "What?"

Chas imitated his behavior. "You sound like a damn chipmunk."

"Sorry."

Walker smiled. Those two were meant for each other.

In the late afternoon, they headed back on the trail. More hoofed animals emerged from the hills—a jackrabbit-sized klipspringer and a handsome kudu with yard-long spiraling horns. A female warthog with three piglets in tow raced across the trail in front of Chas. Even he was impressed.

"Startled by warthogs," he said. "I've got a name for my new band."

That evening, they made a fire and shared stories about the day's sightings. Walker found the canned stew extra satisfying and even risked a cup of Cecil's black tea. The caffeine set his insides rumbling, and in the gathering dusk, he got up to relieve himself. Shovel in hand, he picked his way through the thorn trees to a spot overlooking the creek. He scraped a hole in the dirt and dropped his shorts.

Four days in, Walker was getting used to shitting in the bush. In fact, he quite liked it. The squatting position was conducive to relieving oneself. That's the way humans had done it for millenia. The whole process was calming—sitting alone in silence, away from the others, watching the surroundings? When else did he do that?

Movement across the creek caught his eye. The rock outcropping appeared to come alive and flow downhill. It was an animal—a big one with spotted flanks and a long tail. A leopard! It crossed to his side of the creek and disappeared into the bush. He pulled up his pants and raced back to camp.

"Guys, I just saw a leopard!"

The others jumped up.

"Which way?" Schwartzy said.

Cecil, as usual, had to retrieve his gear from the Land Rover, but there was no waiting for him this time. The boys hurried down to the creek bed.

Walker pointed. "He went right in there."

He tiptoed along the bank, peering into the bush. Nothing. The light was fading fast. "He's gone," Walker said.

Cecil arrived with Bolex in hand. "Are you quite sure it was a leopard?" he said. "There are smaller cats around. It was probably a serval."

"No, it was bigger than a serval."

Walker was disappointed that Cecil didn't believe him. It diminished his credibility with the others and made him feel if he alone saw something out of the ordinary, it didn't really count.

Elliot believed him. Back at camp, he asked if it was okay to sleep in the Land Rover.

"Don't be silly," Cecil said.

"But what about the leopard?"

"The leopard, if that's even what it was, is not interested in you. Do you think he's going to pluck you out of your sleeping bag?"

"Why wouldn't he?"

"Humans are not their typical prey. They go after smaller, weaker things—antelope and the like."

Elliot sighed.

"Actually, I do remember one night when I flicked on my headlamp and saw a lion standing not ten yards away," Cecil said. "It was a bit unnerving, but I told him to bugger off, and he went on his way."

Chas frowned. "And this is supposed to make us feel better?"

"Yeah, really," Schwartzy said. "Are we supposed to wait until there's a lion at our doorstep before we do anything?"

The others were clearly afraid, but Walker was not. He was loving this adventure. As darkness descended, he got into his sleeping bag, turned on his flashlight, and read from Thoreau.

I think that I cannot preserve my health and spirits unless I spend four hours a day at least sauntering through the woods and over the hills and fields. When sometimes I am reminded that the mechanics and shopkeepers stay at their shops not only all the forenoon, but all the afternoon, sitting with crossed legs…I think that they may deserve some credit for not having committed suicide long ago.

Chapter 6

Cecil smiled to himself as he drove down the road out of the mountains. He'd gotten some fabulous footage of the Hartmann's zebras, this to go with the shots of the boys racing among the sea lions. He would have loved to have gotten a shot of that leopard, but who knows if that's what Walker actually saw? These boys were not experts on African wildlife, though Walker seemed to know more than the others.

This Alec was still a bit of a thorn in the side. Who comes to Africa without a camera and then complains about being bored? He glanced in the rearview mirror to see the blue Land Rover following.

"Where are we headed again?" Elliot asked.

"Windhoek. We'll be staying with some friends of mine. Christiann and Anna Smuts. Lovely people."

"Are we staying in their garage?"

"I don't think so. They've got a big house with a couple of bedrooms and some couches. We've slept on those in the past."

"Are they cooking us dinner?"

"Is that all you boys think about, soft beds and home-cooked meals?"

These Americans were so spoiled. Walker and Paul showed some genuine interest in the things around them, but the others...

The land became greener as they approached the outskirts of Windhoek, genuine trees rising above the grasslands. Here was a traffic circle planted with palms, and beyond that, a residential area bounded by a pink stucco wall topped with broken glass. Very effective at keeping thieves out.

They entered the downtown, passing by old government offices with scalloped gables and red tile roofs. That was about it for notable architecture. Every other building was an unornamented box. The German developers of this town seemed to have had no more interest in design than they had a sense of humor.

They left the downtown and headed to the upscale suburb of Ludwigsdorf. The low roof of the Smuts' house appeared at the top of a hill.

"I forgot to mention, the Smuts have a pet baboon," Cecil said.

"Will he bring us tea?" Chas said.

"Don't be silly. He's chained to a post in the backyard. You can go up to him, but I don't think he likes to be petted."

Christiann Smuts stood on the doorstep of his rancher, watering the lawn. He had the classic look of an Afrikaner—a tan, chiseled face, and a trim beard and mustache. He wore a khaki shirt and short shorts, thick woolen socks, and boots. He shook Cecil's hand with an iron grip.

"You made good time, ja?"

"No trouble at all. We left the campsite about eight."

Christiann instructed everyone to bring in their gear.

"We've got a bed or a couch for each of you. Take your

pick," he said. "Cecil, we've got your old bedroom made up."

"Lovely. Thanks."

Christiann's wife, Anna, greeted them in a high, sing-songy voice. "Welkom, welkom! Can I get you boys something to drink?"

Cecil stepped into the living room, the walls adorned with the heads of impala and kudu.

"Did you find your zebras?" Christiann asked.

Cecil nodded. "Yes, we had a fantastic sighting. A whole herd strung across the mountain."

"How lucky!"

Alec peered out a window. "Can we see your baboon?" he asked.

"Ja, for sure," Christiann said. "She's out in the backyard. Name's Sheila."

"Passop!" Anna called from the kitchen. Be careful!

Sheila sat in the middle of a circular patch of bare ground that defined the limits as to how far her chain could reach. She was a large animal with coal-black eyes and a long muzzle.

"Stand here just inside the perimeter," Christiann said. "She'll come to inspect you. Stand your ground and try not to show fear."

Cecil stood back as Sheila approached the boys. Starting with Paul, she smelled his hand and looked him in the eye.

Paul stiffened. "Oh, shit! Are you sure she won't bite?"

The baboon moved along the line, sniffing each boy in turn. Before she could reach him, Elliot broke and ran for the back door. In an instant, the baboon lunged after him, bared her teeth, and let loose a fearsome bark.

Christiann laughed. "I told you about that, ja?"

The boys had seen enough. They retreated to the house, where Anna stood waiting with their drinks.

"I saw Sheila give you a scare," she said to Elliot.

"And like an idiot, he ran," Chas said.

"You don't want to do that in the bush, facing a lion or elephant," Christiann said. "You could put the whole group in jeopardy. It's the same with our Blacks, ja? You've got to be tough with them. I run a construction business, and I know."

"How are you tough with them?" Schwartzy asked.

"If one of them gets cheeky with me, I hit him."

"You hit him?"

Christiann formed a fist. "Hard. On top of the head."

"What if he fights back?"

"No one has. Not yet. But there's groups trying to cause trouble."

"What are you going to do if the Blacks rebel all together?" Walker said.

Christiann gazed at him. "Come here. All of you boys."

He opened a closet in the hall and proceeded to take out a number of guns, starting with a pistol.

"That's a .45," he said. "Stop a man dead in his tracks."

He gave the gun to Alec, who turned it over in his hands. "Nice. How does this compare to a .357?"

"Know a bit about guns, do you? They'll both get the job done."

He handed Walker a rifle. "This is a Mauser 30-06."

Walker tilted it from side to side. "Do most White people in South West Africa have a closet full of guns?" he said.

"The smart ones do. You might have heard there's been trouble up in the North. Rebels have been sneaking into the country from camps in Angola."

"SWAPO rebels?" Schwartzy asked.

"SWAPO. PLAN. They go by different names. We'll be ready for them if they come this way."

All this talk made Cecil nervous. "Come, come, boys, let's put the guns away."

Anna chimed in. "Yes, Christiann, put your guns away and get the braai going."

She announced that they had a special meal planned for the group—boerewors, South Africa's trademark sausage! Cecil was familiar with it. Too damn spicy, but he would let the boys judge for themselves.

They gathered on the back lawn, away from the baboon. The view was quite lovely—rolling hills, scattered rooftops, and green lawns amongst the trees. Christiann put the sausages on the grill, and the air filled with a delightful smell. Anna came out with a cheese board and some crackers.

"I might have a gin and tonic when you've got the time," Cecil said.

"Of course," Anna said. "Do the boys drink alcohol?"

"No, I don't allow it," he said.

"They're very polite. You've been having a good time with them, ja?"

"For the most part. I'm having a bit of trouble with Alec there, but he seems to have settled down."

"It's very brave of you to entertain them for a full month, is it?"

"A month and a half, actually."

"Goedheid!"

She went off to fetch his drink. Cecil strolled over to join Christiann at the grill.

"Where are you headed from here?" Christiann asked.

"Up to Etosha."

"Ja. It's marvelous up there. Been trouble along the border, but they've not closed the park."

"I should hope not. These rebels are becoming a bit of a nuisance, aren't they?"

"More than a nuisance. Since Angola became independent, they've become a real threat. They have a base of operations where we can't touch them."

"Bloody wogs."

Anna brought out potato salad and green peppers and set them on a table. Christiann pronounced the boerewors ready. He handed out a double helping to each of the boys.

"I'll just have one, thanks," Cecil said.

Cecil helped himself to potato salad and sat in a lawn chair. As he cut open the sausage, bloody juices streamed out onto his plate. Ooof. The boys, too, were curling up their noses. Chas spat a piece onto his plate. Paul tossed a whole sausage to Sheila.

Christiann turned, saw the baboon eating. "You don't like our boerewors?" he said to the boys.

Elliot blushed. "It's a little spicy."

"How about the rest of you? I've got plenty more."

In the morning, Cecil drove into town to stock up on groceries at the Spar supermarket. Then he and the boys bid the Smuts goodbye and headed out on the road for Etosha National Park. Cecil typically avoided going to national parks. He didn't like to be confined to formal campsites or prohibited from tracking game on foot. But you couldn't come to northern South West Africa without going to

Etosha. The park was enormous—21,000 square miles—flat as a pancake, mostly devoid of trees but full of game. On his dozen or so trips there, he'd seen giraffes, desert oryx, lions, elephants, and black rhinos. It would certainly satisfy the boys' need for photographs.

Cecil sped on through the open countryside, hoping to catch sight of some of the animals that lived outside the park. Here was something—a brown smear in the middle of the road. It could be just dirt or the carcass of a jackrabbit. But just maybe...

He pulled over to the shoulder, waking Chas up from his nap.

"What's going on?" Chas said.

"I need to check something."

He waved Alec to pull over, then strode out into the road and stood over the flattened dung heap. The boys got out of the cars and gathered around.

"This is elephant shit," he exclaimed. "At least a few day's old. You can tell by the dryness of the fibers. Do you see how they fall apart?"

"There are elephants outside the park?" Walker said.

"Yes, they stray out on occasion. Let's keep driving."

Cecil hopped behind the wheel, giddy with excitement. Elephants were his favorite animal, much more interesting than lions or hippos, which typically just lay around during the day. Elephants moved about. They had personality and, in addition, produced something which he, admittedly, was fascinated with—their droppings. Elephant dung had a marvelous variety of consistencies. Older dung was dry and odorless, the contents coming apart in your hands like so many strands of straw. Fresh dung was warm and moist, weighty...

Cecil came over a rise. Here was another pile. This looked good. Very good. He leaped out of the car and hurried into the road. The bocce-ball-sized dung was fully intact. He picked one up and fondled it in his hands.

"This is fresh," he said to the boys. "No more than a day old."

"So, we might see them today?" Elliot said.

"Quite likely." He broke the dung ball apart and examined its contents—all grass, no leaves, typical of this treeless environment.

"You really like playing with that shit, don't you?" Chas said.

"Yes, well..."

Back on the road, a buzz of anticipation filled the air. Walker loaded a new roll of film and screwed on his telephoto lens. Even Chas sat forward in his seat. The evening sun filled the landscape with a golden hue. They rounded a bend.

"There they are!" Chas said. "Son of a bitch!"

The elephants plodded single file down the middle of the road—one, two, three of them. Cecil closed to within a hundred yards and came to a stop. The boys jumped out of the car and fired away with their cameras. Not great shots, just the elephants' rear ends. But there in the road was something really enticing—a pile of steaming dung. He knew he shouldn't do it but couldn't help himself. He crossed the pavement and knelt down.

"Boys!" he cried. "Look at this shit!"

Chapter 7

In the half-hour it took Cecil to drive from the park entrance to the campground, Walker saw more wildlife than he'd seen in the previous week. Giraffes stood like cartoon characters out in the veldt, appearing improbably large with no trees to measure them against. Kori bustards, giant dinosaur-like birds, strode through the grass looking for snakes. Walker's goal was to get photographs of the Big Five—elephant, African buffalo, leopard, lion, and rhinoceros. He'd photographed an elephant before even entering the park, and within a few miles, they'd come on a herd of buffalo. Two down, three to go.

They reached their campground just before sunset. Around a circular drive, a dozen vehicles—some RVs, some cars with tents—were parked beneath the scattered shade trees. People had set up tables and chairs and were busy grilling dinner.

Walker brought out his cot and set it up on the grass. Next door, two adults and a teenage girl sat on lawn chairs. The girl was beautiful—long dark hair, dark eyes, and shapely legs revealed by a pair of very short shorts. Alec saw her, too. He gave her a wave. She waved back.

As soon as the boys had set up camp, Alec made his move. He strode over and introduced himself to the girl and her parents. He was all smiles, the first time on the trip he'd shown that side of himself. He stayed until Cecil called him back for dinner.

"So, what's her name?" Walker said after Alec returned.

"Ulsa. And she's invited me for dinner."

Cecil frowned. "You're not eating with us?"

"Her dad's making hamburgers, so…"

Alec departed, leaving Walker and the others to sit in silence around the campfire. They kept glancing over at the other campsite.

"Why did Alec even come on this trip?" Elliot said. "He doesn't seem interested in anything we do."

"I suspect he may have some quarrel with his parents," Cecil said. "They may have sent him on the trip just to get him out of the house."

"Did you know that beforehand?" Schwartzy said.

"No, his parents were quite nice when I met them, though Alec seemed rather distant during my conversation with them. His father has a different last name, so I'm guessing the man is not his real father."

"There you go," Chas said. "Mommy has a new daddy, and they don't want Alec around."

Walker felt conflicted about his own emotions. On the one hand, he wanted to be loyal to Cecil and the others, to not do anything that would cause jealousy or dissension. On the other, he wished he'd had the courage to approach Ulsa first.

As darkness fell and Alec still did not return, his jealousy turned to self-hatred. It was his fault that he was alone. Again. He took out a harmonica and launched into a plaintive tune.

"That's a good one," Schwartzy said. "Keep it going."

But the cooing and laughter from next door defeated him. He stuffed his harmonica back in his duffle and laid down on his cot. Sleep did not come until late in the night, when Alec finally returned.

The next morning, Cecil announced they would do a driving tour of Etosha Park. Walker made sure to ride with Alec in the blue Land Rover. He wanted as much information as he could get about last night's escapade.

As they headed out across the grassy plain, he posed the question as nonchalantly as he could.

"So, tell me about Ulsa," he said.

Alec shrugged. "What do you want to know?"

"Where she's from. What she's like…"

"She's German. Here with her parents for two weeks."

"How old is she?"

"Sixteen going on twenty. That girl is hot."

"Oh, yeah?"

"She's a good kisser, I'll tell you that much."

"How did you pull that off with her parents around?"

"They were in their camper fucking."

"Seriously?"

"You could hear them through the walls. It was quite the turn-on."

Walker shook his head. His parents would never engage in sex with their kids so close, nor would any parents he knew. This casualness around sex must be a European thing. Was Ulsa also this uninhibited?

They came upon a herd of zebras standing beside the road. These would be the common Plains zebra, as opposed to the Hartmann's zebra. Walker took a few shots. It was cool to see them up close, but in a short time the novelty wore off. Cecil signaled for them to move on.

"So, did Cecil say anything about me staying out?" Alec said.

"Yeah, he was pretty pissed. Are you going to go back over there tonight?" Walker said.

"Why wouldn't I?"

Asshole. He really didn't care about the group.

They came upon other animals—eland, impala, hartebeest. Walker asked Alec to stop so he could photograph each one.

Alec frowned. "Are you going to take a picture of every animal we see? The light's not even good."

"True, but I want to document everything."

"Why bother taking a picture if you're not going to like the result? You can just tell people what you saw."

Walker pondered that. The story he would tell others would definitely be shaped by the photographs he had. Maybe Alec was better off in some respects. His enjoyment of Africa, such as it was, was not based on the need to have a photographic record. Was he, Walker, less alive in the moment because he fussed with his camera? He hoped not.

Around noon, they circled back to the campground. He was relieved to see Ulsa's camper gone, though their table and chairs were still there. They must be out touring the park.

After a lunch of sausage rolls, Walker began a journal, listing the animals he'd seen and recounting Cecil's bizarre fascination with elephant dung. He did not mention Ulsa. As with his photographing animals, maybe if he didn't record his non-encounter with her, he would soon forget about it.

In the late afternoon, they set back on the road. They encountered more of the same animals they'd seen in the morning, with the addition of desert oryx and wildebeest. Walker was growing disappointed they had not seen any big cats, specifically lion or leopard. Up ahead, Cecil pulled over to the side of the road. He pointed out the window toward the seemingly empty grassland.

"What's he looking at?" Elliot said.

Walker raised up in his seat. Two hundred feet in, a pair of ears protruded above the grass.

"There's something lying in there," he said.

Another pair of ears appeared, and then a head with distinctive yellow eyes.

"Lions!" he said. "There's four of them, one male and a couple of females."

Schwartzy and Chas got out of the red Land Rover and started taking pictures. Cecil must have given the okay, so Walker got out as well. Hoping for a better view, he climbed onto the hood of the car. He took a dozen shots, but they weren't great. The lions remained hunkered down, enjoying their afternoon nap.

"I wish they'd stand up," Elliot said.

Alec leaned over and picked up a baseball-sized rock from the side of the road. "You want them to stand up? I'll make them stand up."

He heaved the rock, hitting the big male right on its side. The lion jumped to his feet.

"Jesus!" Walker said. "What the fuck are you doing?"

A car door slammed. Cecil stormed over. "I saw what you did, Alec. Are you out of your mind?"

Alec shrugged. "Elliot said he wanted a better shot."

"Throwing rocks at a lion? You could get us all tossed out of the park."

"Sorry."

"You bloody well ought to be. One more incident like this, and I'm sending you home."

They returned to the campground to find Ulsa sitting out on a lawn chair. She waved expectantly at Alec, but he just slumped onto his cot with his hand over his face. She looked to Walker and turned her palms up, indicating that she didn't understand what was going on.

Screwing up his courage, Walker strode over and introduced himself. "Alec got in a bit of trouble today, so he's not in a talkative mood," he said.

"Oh, no. What happened?"

"He threw a rock at a lion."

"At a lion?"

Walker explained that this was the third time Alec had screwed up, and that if he did one more thing, Cecil would send him home. Walker hoped these revelations might cause Ulsa to lose interest in the guy. Sure enough, she invited him to stay.

"I'm jealous of you guys," she said. "Out on your own."

"You don't like being with your parents?"

"It's okay."

He asked where she'd been, where she was going next.

"We're going to Vic Falls after this," she said.

"Seriously, we're going there, too!"

She touched his arm. "That's wonderful! I might see you!"

Walker glanced back at the group. They were all watching him, Cecil in particular.

"I'd better go back," he said. "Nice meeting you."

"Nice to meet you, too."

Alec scowled as he came back to camp. "Trying to steal my girl?" he said.

"Hey, fuck you. She's not your personal possession."

"Boys, boys," Chas said. "Be cool."

"Yes, I didn't bring you all here to chase girls," Cecil said. He tossed the dried pea soup into a pot of boiling water and handed Walker a can of stew.

"Open that for me," he said.

Darkness set in. The boys ate in silence. After a time, Alec stood and looked in Ulsa's direction. She and her parents sat at a table playing cards under the light of a lantern.

Cecil frowned. "Don't even think about it," he said.

Chapter 8

The night of the rock-throwing incident, Cecil could barely sleep. Alec was driving him batty, and the prospect of putting up with the boy for another three weeks was utterly depressing. Cecil wasn't much of a drinker, but he sorely wished he had a bottle of whiskey to calm himself down.

The following day, they sighted an ostrich standing just off the road. The boys got some good photos, which put them in good spirits, all except Alec, who continued to sulk. Once again, he snuck off to the girl's campsite after dinner. Rather than make an issue of it, Cecil let Alec go. No point in picking a fight.

On the last day, he was driving with Walker and Elliot out of the park when he sighted a pangolin crossing the road. This was a comparatively rare creature, much like an armadillo but twice the size. He'd only seen a few pangolins and never successfully filmed one. This could be his chance. He hit the brakes and pulled over to the side of the road.

"What the hell was that?" Paul said, jumping out of Alec's car.

"A pangolin. Quick, see if you can find him while I get my camera."

Cecil retrieved his Bolex while the boys searched through the grass.

"He's over here!" Paul yelled. "He's headed toward a big hole."

"That's his burrow!" Cecil said. "Can you stop him from going in?"

Several of the boys jumped in front of the pangolin, blocking its forward progress. Cecil arrived, set up his tripod and readied his camera, but the creature had curled into a ball, showing only its scaly back.

He peered through his viewfinder. "Bloody hell. This is not a good shot."

"How long is it going to stay like that?" Paul said.

"No telling.

Minutes passed. The creature would not unroll. Finally, Cecil called it quits.

"Alright, let's move on. It's not going to move while we're around."

He packed up his tripod and camera and got back in the car. He started down the road, glancing in his rearview mirror to make sure the others were coming. Damnit, Alec was still standing in the grass. What on earth was he doing? Good God, he was pissing on the pangolin!

Cecil slammed on the brakes, put the Rover in reverse, and backed up. He threw open the door and stormed up to Alec as the boy was zipping his fly.

"Are you out of your bloody mind?" He spun Alec around and pushed him towards his car. "You are done. I'm sending you home!"

After leaving the boys at the campground, Cecil drove to park headquarters and put a call through to Christiann. He explained the situation and asked could they please stay at his house for a few days while he arranged to send Alec home?

"Absolutely," Christiann said. "I'll expect you this evening."

The drive back to Windhoek was excruciating. His passengers, Walker and Paul, were uncharacteristically silent the entire time. He glanced constantly in the mirror to make sure Alec wasn't straying. Upon arrival at the Smuts, he had to wait until the boys were ensconced in the TV room before he dared open his mouth.

"This boy, Alec, is driving me out of my bloody fucking mind," he said to Christiann. "I've got to send him home."

"You're right, man. You've got to put your foot down with these types. Let's get on the line with Lufthansa. They've got a daily flight to London."

"Oh, good."

"You say he lives in New York?"

"Yes. Just outside the city."

"They'll find him a connection."

Christiann got an agent on the line. Yes, they had a flight to London with a connection to New York but did not have a seat for two days.

"Do you mind our waiting here?" Cecil said.

"Not at all. The ticket is twelve hundred rands."

Cecil waved his hand. "I'll pay it. Anything to get him out of my hair."

Christiann booked the flight. Cecil collapsed in a chair.

"I'll have to go to the bank and get some money. And I'll need to send a telegram to his parents."

"We'll do all that tomorrow."

"What am I going to do about driving the other Land Rover? None of the boys is old enough for an international driver's license."

Christiann pondered that. "I know a travel agent in town. He may be able to find you a driver."

"That would be marvelous."

"You need to get some rest."

"I can't sleep. I'm too pissed by all this."

Christiann furrowed his brow. "Let me get you something. Anna sometimes has trouble sleeping."

He came back with a blue pill and held it out for Cecil to see. "Little bit of Valium."

"Gosh, I've never taken one of these before."

"They work quite well. I promise you'll sleep."

Cecil downed the pill with a cup of water. "You'll see to the boys?" he said.

"They're downstairs watching the telly. Come on to your bed."

Cecil followed Christiann into the guest bedroom. The man was an absolute savior. Cecil turned and hugged him. "I'm so grateful to you."

Christiann patted him on the back. "Cheers. We'll get this all sorted out."

※

Cecil awoke to sunlight streaming through the shades. Where was he? Oh, yes, it all came back in a rush. He glanced at his watch. Ten AM! He pulled on his clothes, matted down his hair in front of the mirror, and hurried into the living room. Anna was in the kitchen fixing a meal.

"There you are," she said. "I thought you'd never wake up."

"That pill absolutely knocked me out. I've never slept so late in my life!"

"You must have needed it."

"Where is everyone?"

"Christiann took them to town to see a museum and have a bit of lunch."

He felt a moment of panic. Someone else was taking charge of his group. "Alec went with them?"

"Don't worry. Christiann will keep him in line. Now, sit down and relax. Can I fix you some breakfast? Some toast? An egg?"

"That would be lovely. Poached, if you don't mind. And I'll have some tea."

He settled in at the breakfast table. "I can't tell you how grateful I am. I've never had this happen before."

"It sounds like you've had a rough time of it. What's wrong with that boy?"

"I wish I could tell you."

He picked up a copy of the newspaper and scanned the headlines. The lead story was about the transitional government of Angola falling apart within months of the country's declaration of independence from Portugal. Three factions—one backed by the Soviet Union, one backed by South Africa, and one backed by Zaire—were vying for power. Civil war was at hand in the country right next door.

"Have you read this about Angola?" Cecil said.

Anna sighed. "Ja. It's a horrible mess. Next thing you know, we'll have a communist country next door."

"The Africans are utterly incapable of running a country," Cecil said. "We've seen that a dozen times. That's why I refuse to call this country 'Namibia.' What does it even mean?"

"And the Angolans are letting SWAPO set up bases across the river from us. You've heard about that, ja?"

"Ridiculous."

"Fortunately, SADF has taken over border security from the police," Anna said. "They'll teach those boys a lesson."

"'Sadif'? Is that what you call the South African Defense Force?" Cecil said.

"Ja. Easier than saying S, A, D, F."

After breakfast, Anna announced she would take Cecil downtown to visit the bank and the travel agent. He insisted he could drive himself, but she warned that Valium could have lingering effects.

"Well, I wouldn't mind the company," he said. "And it'd be nice to have a woman along."

As they headed into town, Anna asked him more about Alec. Why was he behaving this way?

"He must have been through something lately," he said. "I believe his parents are divorced. The father I met has a different last name."

Anna nodded. "You need to have a man in the house that a child respects. A new father rarely works out if a child is in his teens."

Cecil stared out the window. "It's not in my nature to be strict with these boys."

"Your father wasn't strict with you?"

"He was quite absent for most of my childhood. My mother was the strict one, but with me, she didn't need to be. I was quite the obedient child."

They arrived at Barclay's Bank. Cecil took out thirteen hundred rands in cash, enough to cover Alec's plane ticket and a cab from JFK to Greenwich. Then, it was on to the travel agent.

Piet De Beers was a friendly chap. He assured Cecil he could come up with a driver, a service they regularly arranged for tourists going to Etosha Park.

"I'll need him for three weeks," Cecil said. "We're going from here to Vic Falls, then on to Mana Pools, and back down to Cape Town."

Piet frowned. "That's far. I'll have to add bus fare from Cape Town to get my driver back here."

"Yes, I suspected as much."

"Are you staying in any lodges? If so, we'll need to make arrangements for him."

By that, he understood that the driver would be Black.

"No, we sleep outside on cots. I've got an extra one and a sleeping bag, as well."

Piet thumbed through his file. "I've got just the chap for you. Patrick Hangula, a real good boy. He's driven a number of people up to Etosha."

Piet handed him the file. A smiling face stared out from the page—dark black skin, round face. A member of the dominant Ovambo tribe.

"Fantastic! Oh, what a relief!"

Chapter 9

Patrick Hangula sat on a three-legged stool in the tree-shaded courtyard of his home in Katutura, Windhoek's all-Black township. His mother, Namutenya, bent over a charcoal-fired stove, stirring the stew in the Potjeikos pot. Patrick took out his wallet and counted the earnings from his latest excursion, disappointed with the tip given by his British clients—a mere five percent. Germans were better tippers, though he had no love for their condescending attitudes.

The gate creaked, and in walked Josiah, his older brother. Josiah threw his hat in the dirt and plunked down on the empty stool.

"My fucking boss," Josiah said. "I want to kill him."

Namutenya scowled. "Josiah! Watch your mouth!"

"What happened?" Patrick said.

"He hit me."

"Your boss hit you? With his fist?"

"A slap. On the back of the head."

"What have you done to deserve this?" Namutenya said.

"Nothing. He called me a lazy kaffir."

"Because you were sitting around?"

"He complained because the cement mixer had not been cleaned. That was not my fault. I was not the only one to use it. But I was the one he told to chip it out. I told him to bugger off."

Patrick gasped. "You told him that? You will get fired!"

Josiah was silent.

"Did you get fired?" Patrick said. "Tell me, brother."

"I did. But I don't regret it. It's time we stand up to the Boer."

Namutenya threw her hands up in despair. "Now, what will you do? No one will hire you."

"I'm joining the SWAPO combatants. I'm going to fight for our freedom. Now that the Portuguese are leaving Angola, we'll be free to use that as a base."

"You would become a soldier?" Patrick said.

"Yes. You should join, too."

Patrick looked away.

"Ya, you don't want to risk your precious job," Josiah said. "Driving tourists around to stare at gemsbok."

"It's a good job."

"As long as you don't speak your mind. When will you seek real freedom, brother?"

"He has money in his pocket," Namutenya said. "That's freedom."

Patrick was silent. He believed in SWAPO's commitment to independence. The news from Angola hinted that resistance to the White minority regime could be fruitful. But he was afraid of the South Africans. They'd been running Namibia since the 1920s. Their defense force was made up of professionals with the latest weapons. He dared not try to talk his brother out of joining the resistance, but he was a long way from doing so himself.

Two days later, Josiah announced that he had spoken with a SWAPO recruiter. He would be leaving the next morning to begin training. Patrick cried, holding his brother in his arms.

"What will I do if you get killed?"

Now, tears came to Josiah's eyes. "You will take care of our mother. And yourself. It's best that you keep your job. She would be lost without you."

"Where are they sending you? Will you write us?"

"They didn't say, but I'm guessing I'll be sent to Lubango. I will try to write. If you need to reach me, contact the recruiter."

Josiah handed him a piece of paper with an address on it. "Don't show this to Meme. Have her send anything through you."

Patrick nodded and gave him a final hug. "Be safe, my brother."

※

In the morning, Piet drove Patrick in his bakkie to meet his new clients. Klein Windhoek was a White man's neighborhood, big houses with green lawns and shady trees, protected by high walls topped with broken glass. Two Land Rovers, one red and one blue, were parked in the driveway. Piet parked on the street, and they crossed the lawn, the grass underfoot like the softest carpet. Piet knocked on the door, and a White woman answered. She introduced herself as Anna.

"Let me get Cecil. Would you like to come in?" she said to Piet.

"Thanks, I'll wait here," Piet said.

A tall, slump-shouldered White man appeared whom Piet introduced as Cecil.

"He's down from England," Piet said. "He'll be your boss."

Cecil asked if Patrick would like to see the car he'd be driving, a blue Land Rover of 1960s vintage.

"Yes, I'm familiar with these," Patrick said.

"Good," Cecil said. "Let me get the boys. You'll enjoy them, I think."

One by one, four boys came out the door. They each walked up and shook his hand, a politeness he didn't expect.

"They're all Americans," Cecil said by way of explanation.

Patrick hadn't met many Americans. He assumed they must be like all the other Whites, but maybe not.

"Yes, well, let's get going," Cecil said. "We've got a lot of ground to cover."

Patrick retrieved his duffle bag and put it in the blue Rover.

"See you in three weeks," Piet said. "Good luck."

Piet's words reminded Patrick it would be a long time before he heard any news of Josiah, a long time that he would be in the company of strangers.

As the boys loaded their gear, Cecil took out a map and went over their route.

"Right. We'll be heading east across the Kalahari today. I hope to get as far as Ghanzi."

"Yes, I know this route."

"We should arrive at Vic Falls late in the day on Wednesday. You've been there, I assume."

He had. He was also familiar with the next leg to Mana Pools National Park, but he'd never driven from there all the way down to Cape Town.

"Are you clear about this?" Cecil said.

"Yes, baas."

"You're to stay behind me at all times. Flash your lights if you need to stop."

"Yes, baas."

With that, they got underway. Two boys rode with him, one named Paul or Schwartzy and the other named Walker.

Paul got in the front seat. "Great to have you, man," Paul said. "Our last driver was a real jerk."

"He was one of your friends?" Patrick said.

Walker snorted. "Not any more."

Patrick chose not to ask any more about this person. He started the engine and followed Cecil out into the street.

"You've got to double-clutch between first and second," Paul said.

"Yes, Mr. Cecil explained this to me."

"And don't ever pass him," Walker said. That set both boys laughing.

They headed out of Windhoek and east toward Gobabis. No sooner were they on the road than the boys started peppering him with questions.

"What tribe are you from?" Paul wanted to know.

"I am Ovambo. We are Bantu speakers."

"Ovambo," Walker said. "You're the biggest tribe in this country, right?"

"Yes, Ovambo is the largest."

"You were here before the Whites," Paul said.

"Yes, we have been here many centuries. We and the Herero."

"Were you the original inhabitants, or were those the Bushmen?" Walker asked.

"The San people were first, but they are, how do you say, wandering people. They did not own land. The Bantu brought cows and built farms."

"I heard the Bantu drove the Bushmen out into the Kalahari," Paul said. "Is that right?"

"Yes, this is true. Some of them work here now. On the farms and in the cities."

This talk made Patrick very uncomfortable. None of his clients had ever brought up these events from the past. He knew about them, of course, but what was safe to say?

They approached a truck full of laborers in sky-blue uniforms. The men stared at them, unsmiling.

"What's up with these people?" Paul said.

"These are contract laborers," Patrick said. "They are going to work on the farms."

"For White people?"

"Yes, for White people. They must wear these uniforms and a wristband with their number on it."

"Like prisoners, huh?"

"No, they are not prisoners."

A long silence followed. They *were* prisoners, in a way. The workers could not break their contract, or they would risk being arrested and punished. It was a system the Africans despised.

The truck turned off onto a dirt road, and Patrick breathed easy.

"You boys are all Americans?" he said.

"All except Cecil," Paul said. "He's our resident British colonialist."

That was a strange thing for a White boy to say. Walker asked if he got many American clients.

"Not many. British, yes. And Germans."

"Oh, yeah? How do you like the Germans?" Paul said.

"They are nice."

"Some of them are. Especially the girls, right, Walker?"

Walker laughed at this. Clearly, they had met some German girls.

At noon, they arrived in Gobabis. Cecil pulled into a petrol station with a restaurant where they planned to have lunch. Patrick had been here before. There was outdoor seating for the drivers under the shade of a palm tree. He recognized two drivers, Lazarus and Festus, seated at a table.

"Welcome, Patrick," Lazarus said. "Come sit down."

Patrick took a seat while Cecil led the boys inside. Paul turned around at the door. "Hey, Patrick, come sit inside with us."

"No, I am fine here."

Cecil said something to Paul, who shook his head in disgust. Paul did not know the system.

Festus leaned in. "Who are your clients?"

"The baas man is British. The boys are American."

Patrick related how he had been hired at the last minute because one of the boys, the only one old enough to drive, had been sent home for bad behavior.

"All the way back to America?" Lazarus said. "It must have been serious."

"I don't know what this boy has done."

He relayed the group's itinerary—Vic Falls, on to Mana Pools, then down to Cape Town.

Lazarus grew wide-eyed. "Eeee, it is far! How long will you be out?"

"Three weeks."

"What lodges are you staying in?"

"No lodges. We are camping out."

"Every night? Oh, is a shame. Be careful of the lions."

"And the hyenas," Festus said. He and Lazarus had a good laugh.

"I hope they tip you well," Lazarus said.

"I don't think the boys have much money. And the leader is British."

"Agh, you'll be lucky to get five percent!"

More laughter followed, but in fact, Patrick was worried. He was hoping for a big tip to bring home to his mother.

After lunch, they got back on the road, reaching the border with Botswana in less than an hour. The White officer at the Namibian post asked Patrick for his travel papers and scrutinized them closely. Africans needed special permission to travel outside of the country, especially since the troubles had begun. The Black officer at the Botswanan post merely glanced at his papers, then waved him on.

Botswana had been independent since 1966, a free country with a democratically elected government, but it was poor. The paved road ended at the border. There would be no services for hundreds of kilometers. Ahead lay the Kalahari Desert, an endless expanse of sand with a sparse covering of tawny grass. No water. No shade.

The boys stared out at the treeless landscape.

"Are there still some Bushmen out here?" Walker asked.

"The !Gubi, yes. We may see them."

Patrick gripped the steering wheel as the tires squirmed through the deep sand. Several hours along, a rounded shelter appeared beside the road.

"Here is one of their dwellings!" he said. "It's made of twigs."

Paul aimed his camera out the open window. "Can you slow down?"

The shelter was barely waist high, but the people who used them were small, and they always sat on the ground. This one appeared to be abandoned, but after some miles, they saw another with a gutted antelope hanging in the entry. A five-foot-tall man emerged to watch them pass. He was bare-chested and carried a tiny bow and arrow.

Walker grew excited. "These people are really doing it," he said to Paul. "They live completely off the land. No possessions except for what they carry on their backs."

"That is too cool," Paul said.

Patrick reflected on his life back in Oshakati, his ancestral home. His relatives were cattle herders, and he still loved to travel back there, to talk of the weather and the health of the cows, to be away from the harsh gaze of the White man. These !Gubi were lacking in material wealth, but they were, indeed, free in some ways.

In the late afternoon, they reached the trading post at Ghanzi. The post was run by a White man, but dozens of !Gubi were gathered outside. As Patrick slowed to a halt, the boys jumped out and were immediately surrounded. The !Gubi thrust ostrich shell beads at them, and loincloths made of porcupine quills. Walker spied a man with a bow and quiver filled with arrows.

"I want to buy this," he said, pointing to the weapons. "How much?"

"Fifty," the man said.

"Fifty rands? How about thirty?"

The man hesitated. "Forty."

Walker reached for his wallet and peeled off the bills. The man handed him the weapons.

"Be careful you do not touch the tips of the arrows," Patrick said. "They may have poison on them."

"Yeah, I heard about that. I'm going to put it in the car."

After purchasing their share of items from the !Gubi, the boys went into the trading post. The wooden walls were lined with shelves crammed with all manner of goods—tins of Spam, second-hand clothes, spools of wire. Cecil stood at the counter talking to the owner, an old White man with deeply wrinkled skin, milky blue eyes, and thin lips.

"I was wondering if you'd still be here," Cecil said to the man. "It's been quite a few years."

"You've brought another crop of boys?" the man said.

"Yes, it looks like they bought everything they could off the Bushmen."

"I've got a few things they might like."

The man showed the boys a stack of animal skins.

"This is impala," he said. "Makes a fine rug."

Elliot took it in hand. "How much is it?"

"One hundred rands."

"I'd like one."

Paul lifted a blanket of stitched-together skins. "What's this?"

"A jackal skin kaross," the man said. "Three hundred for that one."

Patrick shook his head. The prices were steep, but the boys readily opened their wallets. They had more money than he'd imagined. By the time they were finished, each of them had a rug or kaross to go with their weapons and crafts.

Cecil called them back to the cars. "Come on, boys, we have a ways to go."

That evening, they camped beneath a lone acacia tree, its wide, flat crown like a big umbrella planted in the sand. The boys found enough fallen branches to make a small fire, which they huddled around as darkness fell. Walker brought out the bow and arrow set he'd purchased. Chas asked to see the bow, little more than a bent stick and a string made of animal gut.

"This thing looks pretty feeble," Chas said. "I wouldn't think you could kill anything with it. Maybe a dung beetle."

"All that is necessary is for the arrow to penetrate the animal's hide, then the poison goes to work." Patrick said. "They track the animal until it dies. Sometimes it takes days."

Chas snorted. "What a life."

"It sounds like a pretty good life to me," Walker said. "They're out walking the land every day. They get to use every sense we were evolved to use."

"I'll bet we'll live a lot longer than they will," Chas said.

As the fire died, Patrick began to worry. He'd guided other clients on safari, but he'd never slept outside in just a cot with no walls to protect him from the wild animals that lurked in the dark.

"Baas, do you have a gun?" he asked Cecil.

"No, I never carry a gun. Why should I have a gun?"

"Animals may come. They may smell us."

"I've slept out in the bush for decades. I've never been attacked."

That was little comfort to Patrick. Darkness fell and

the fire dwindled. He climbed into his sleeping bag, imagining what might be lurking just beyond the firelight. Sure enough, out of the dark came an eerie call. "*WooOOOH. WooOOOh.*"

"What the hell is that?" one of the boys said.

"Is a hyena!" Patrick said.

The animal was close—maybe fifty meters. He pictured the ugly beast circling the camp—the head of a dog, the mangy body, and short hind legs. "*WooOOOH! WooOOOH!*" Did the others not fear this animal? They all seemed to be giggling. But this was the sound of a ghost, the dead warning the living.

Chapter 10

Josiah boarded the bus in Katutura carrying a small suitcase that held everything he was allowed to bring—three pairs of trousers, three shirts, five underpants, five pairs of stockings, one toothbrush, and one tube of toothpaste. In his pocket, he held twenty U.S. dollars in cash. If the bus was stopped and searched by the police, he was to say he was going to Rundu to visit a relative.

Rundu was a small town on the border between Namibia and Angola. Though he had not been given any specifics by his SWAPO contact, he guessed that it was here that he would cross the Kavango River into Angola to begin his training as a soldier with the armed wing of SWAPO—the People's Liberation Army of Namibia, better known as PLAN. Upon his arrival at the bus station, he was to look for a cab bearing the name Gemsbok Taxi on the door. He was to tell the driver, "Take me to my grandmother's house."

The day-long drive from Windhoek was nerve-wracking. There were roadblocks at Otjiwarongo, Otavi, and Grootfontein, where the police boarded the bus and questioned the male passengers. Where are you going? What is your grandmother's name? Give me her address. He would wither in front of the White man's stare. They had conditioned all Africans to feel that way.

When the bus pulled out of Grootfontein, Josiah finally relaxed. The sun was sinking low over the treeless landscape. It seemed no one lived out here—African, White, or Colored.

Just before dark, the bus entered the outskirts of Rundu. People were out strolling the streets, enjoying the cool temperatures. Signs of struggle were entirely absent. As the bus pulled into the petrol station where Josiah was to exit, he spotted a police officer scanning the arriving passengers, a big Afrikaaner slapping a baton against his open palm. Sure enough, the man flagged him as he got off the bus.

"Come over here," the man said. "Let me see your identification."

Josiah controlled his trembling hand enough to get ahold of his wallet.

The man studied his ID. "From Windhoek? Do you have travel papers?"

Josiah took out his travel papers.

"What is your business in Rundu?"

"I am here to see my grandmother. She is ill."

"Open up your case."

Josian set the suitcase on the ground and opened the latches. The policeman went through his clothes.

"Planning a long stay?"

"Just a week, then I must go back to my job."

The policeman sent him on his way.

At the curb, Josiah searched the line of cars. Parked across the street was a cab with Gemsbok Taxi on the door.

Should he go to it, or would this be a trap? He glanced over his shoulder. The policeman was searching another man's luggage. He hurried across the street and knocked on the door of the cab.

The driver, a Black man, lowered the window.

"I'm here to see my grandmother," Josiah said.

"Get in," the driver commanded.

As the cab pulled away from the station, the driver eyed him in the rearview mirror.

"Did you have a good trip?" he said.

"Yes. It was no trouble until I arrived here. A policeman flagged me down and searched my luggage."

"That's normal. They are searching all men since the start of the year."

It was now full-on dark. The driver entered a township and stopped in front of an unlit house.

"This is your stop. Knock on the door and tell them your name."

"What do I owe you?"

"Nothing. Be safe, comrade."

This was the first time he'd heard the word "comrade." He knew it was a trademark of communist freedom movements. The Soviet Union was backing many such movements in Africa, including those in Angola, and though PLAN was not avowedly communist, its leaders identified with the notion of class struggle. In South Africa's mind, this Soviet involvement gave them justification for continued governance of Namibia, as well as for fighting PLAN.

If Josiah expected to be received with open arms, he was sorely disappointed. As soon as he entered the house, he was directed to a room with a table and a bare light bulb hanging from the ceiling. Three men sat at the table, none smiling. He offered his hand but was told to sit down.

"Let me see your ID," said the one in the middle. He studied the card and handed it to his compatriots. "You are from Windhoek?"

"Yes, sir."

"I think you are an agent. Sent by SADF."

He couldn't believe his ears. "No, sir, I am not. My people are Kwanyama from Oshakati."

"You left a good job to come here?"

"I was fired. My boss hit me, and I cursed him back."

"That's what you say. Perhaps that was arranged."

"No, sir! You can ask my brother. He was present when I came home."

"Give me your brother's address."

"I can do that, but he is on safari. There's no way to reach him for several weeks."

He thought to mention his mother but did not want to get her involved in this. There was no telling what she might say if she was afraid.

"Take him back," the man said.

Josiah was terrified he would be sent back to the roadblock at the petrol station, but instead, the two other men led him to a room with a cot and wash basin. They told him he was to sleep there and to not leave the house unless ordered.

"Am I a prisoner?"

"No, but you are not to leave."

"May I have some food? I have only had a sandwich on the bus."

One man left and came back with a quarter loaf of

hard bread and a glass of water. "This is all we have. You will get some more in the morning."

***

A day later, Josiah was ushered out of the house. During that time, he was joined by another man, Dominic, who, like him, had volunteered to fight for Namibia's independence. Under cover of darkness, they boarded another vehicle and were driven out of town. They were only told they would be transported across the border into Angola and, once there, taken to a training camp in Lubango, a city safely inland.

In the past year, PLAN combatants had succeeded in killing a number of policemen in hit-and-run attacks from across the border. This prompted the South African Defense Force to establish a five-mile-wide buffer strip along the border where they controlled all movement. Periodic roadblocks were set up. Vehicles were searched, and passengers who couldn't provide good reason for being in the area were subject to arrest and imprisonment.

In the dead of night, Josiah and Dominic were directed into a van with bench seats that were lifted to reveal hidden compartments underneath. Josiah protested he couldn't fit in the coffin-like space, but the driver told him it was either that or go home. He lowered himself down, head on hard metal, arms to his face, and felt the seat close over his body. He lay this way for half an hour, unable to move, as the van rumbled along a gravel road.

"Dominic, are you there?" he whispered.

"Yes, I am here."

"I can't breathe. How long do you think we will drive?"

"Don't panic, my friend. Breathe slowly."

Finally, the vehicle pulled to a halt. The seats were raised, and Josiah and Dominic were freed from their coffins. The door slid open. A figure emerged from the roadside.

"Come with me," he said. "Bring your cases, but do not bump them against the rocks."

Under a moonless sky, they walked over the barren ground to the banks of the Kavango River. There, another man waited with a dugout canoe. Josiah and Dominic were told to wade out until the water was over their ankles.

"Can I take off my shoes?" Josiah asked.

"No."

He waded out, set his case in the canoe, and got in behind the bow paddler. The stern man climbed in, and they started across the river. Immediately, they were immersed in blackness, the only sound the dripping of water from the paddles.

Dominic shifted his weight, causing the canoe to wobble.

"Do not tip the canoe, or we will be food for the crocodiles," one said.

"There are crocodiles in this river?" Josiah asked.

"Big ones. Twenty feet. That's for real."

Josiah had seen videos of these monsters exploding from the depths and dragging full-grown wildebeest into the river. A man would stand no chance against them. And he couldn't even swim.

The river was wide, with no shoreline in sight. Suddenly, the canoe ground to a halt. The bowman stepped out.

"Go to the forest straight ahead," he said. "A man will be waiting. Welcome to Angola."

Chapter 11

The Kalahari behind him, Cecil steered his Land Rover into the heart of Vic Falls Town. He drove between jacaranda trees and sidewalks filled with tourists. The whitewashed buildings glowed in the sun. Such a lovely town.

At the city center, they passed the statue of Cecil Rhodes striding forth atop a granite pedestal.

"Who's this?" Paul asked.

"That's Cecil Rhodes, founder of Rhodesia," Cecil said.

"He found it? What was it before?"

"Don't be silly. He was head of De Beers Mining Company and Prime Minister of the Cape Colony. He made the country what it is."

Cecil drove on east of town and arrived at the campground abutting the Zambezi River. This was a formal campground with numbered spaces, public toilets, and picnic tables. After checking in with the campground host, he drove to their assigned spot. Virtually every other one was taken, a camper or van of some sort parked in the gravel drive.

Chas stepped out and surveyed the campsite. "Is that a real shitter?" he said of the public bathroom.

"Yes, it's just for you, Chas. Warm water and toilet paper."

The blue Rover pulled up. Walker stepped out from the passenger seat, looking bleary-eyed.

"Isn't this marvelous?" Cecil said to him.

Walker shook his head. "Nine hours drive. That's too much."

"Come, come. Don't be a downer."

A voice rang out from the campsite next door. "Hey, you guys!"

Oh, dear. It was the German girl from Etosha Park.

Walker's face lit up. "Ulsa!"

He strode over and gave her a rather affectionate hug. With Alec gone, it was his turn to play Romeo.

Cecil set about unloading his gear, as did the others. By the time they finished, Walker was still jabbering on with Ulsa.

Cecil called, "Are you planning on joining us?"

Walker broke off the conversation and returned immediately. A good boy that, the best of the lot. Cecil had been thinking for some time that he needed one of the boys to accompany him on his attempt to find Livingstone's initials. If they were to wade across the Zambezi, the boy would have to be athletic, brave, and trustworthy.

He pulled Walker aside. "I may have a special mission for you tomorrow," he said.

"What's that?"

"Do you remember my talking about Livingstone carving his initials in a tree on an island in the Zambezi River, just above the falls?"

"Yes."

"I want you to help me find them."

"Me?"

"You're the one I trust the most. If we can manage to find the tree and make a cast of the initials, it would be quite something. You'd be famous, actually."

Walker looked both enthralled and dubious. "What's involved?"

From his pocket, Cecil produced a map of the falls. Upstream of the cataract, the map showed the Zambezi braiding around several islands, one of which sat on the very edge of the precipice.

Cecil tapped his finger on the map. "That's the island right there."

"You're kidding me?"

"I'm not."

The path to the Falls ran parallel to the Zambezi River, but the view of the river was blocked by a thick band of trees and a progressively heavy mist thrown up by the falling water. It was an otherworldly environment, with baboons emerging from the forest to feed on the grassy verge and seek handouts from tourists. The boys paused to take photos, but Cecil had no time for that. It was the Falls he was after.

Victoria Falls was the largest waterfall in the world, more than a mile wide and twice the height of Niagara. It wasn't a continuous curtain, however, but rather a series of falls divided by islands that ran right to the edge. The other feature unique to Victoria Falls was that it didn't spill into a river running straight out from the falls. Rather, it plunged into a narrow crevice that sent the current at right angles, emptying out at one end. The trail they followed ran right out along the edge of that crevice, allowing one to stare straight into the face of the falls for nearly its entire length.

As they neared the turn, the ground itself shook from the force of falling water. A plume of mist shot in the air, filled with the pungent smell of wet earth. Tourists coming back along the trail clutched their soaking jackets.

"It's quite damp!" one shouted. "Be forewarned."

And here it was. The boys froze at the sight of the first cataract.

"Holy shit!"

"Goddamn!"

Mosi-oa-Tunya, the natives called it—The Smoke that Thunders. A lovely name, though Livingstone properly named it after the reigning Queen of England. Cecil waited as the boys fired away with their cameras. Then he urged them on with the promise of a more impressive view ahead.

The main cataract was wider than Niagara, with a double rainbow arcing across its face. There, perched at the very edge, was a wooded island, the one described by Livingstone in his letter. Cecil studied the canopy for the tell-tale shape of a baobab tree—smooth-barked, tall, and branchless except at the very top, often described as looking like a tree planted upside down. At this distance, he couldn't clearly identify a baobab among the densely packed trees, but he was sure it was there. He could feel its presence.

He called Walker over and spoke above the roar. "Do you see that island in the middle? That's the one."

Walker followed his point. "Are you sure? How the hell did he get there?"

"Some natives paddled him in a canoe from upstream, but I think we can get there by wading."

"Are you serious?"

"Yes, the river is quite shallow this time of year. We'll have to study it from above."

Paul noticed them conversing. "What are you guys talking about?" he said.

Walker pointed out the island where Livingstone reputedly carved his initials into a tree. "Cecil wants to wade out there to see if he can find it."

Paul laughed. "Are you shitting me?"

"We're going to check it out."

"What do you mean 'we'?"

"He wants me to come with him."

"You?" Paul stared at Cecil.

"I can only take one of you," Cecil said. "Walker's quite sure-footed, I've noticed."

"Right. Sure-footed," Paul said.

As they followed the trail back towards camp, Cecil suggested they take a look at the river upstream of the falls. By now, all the boys were in on it. They poked through the forest until they reached a narrow channel across from which was another wooded island.

Cecil took out his map. "I was afraid of this," he said. "We can't see Livingstone's island from above. The river splits into several channels. But you see the water is quite shallow. We'll just have to push our way through until we get to the main channel."

"I don't know," Walker said. "Looks pretty risky."

"How do you think Livingstone felt?" Cecil said. "He

faced untold numbers of obstacles."

That evening, Cecil built a fire with wood purchased at the camp headquarters. Walker asked if he could invite Ulsa over. It was polite of him to ask, so Cecil said yes. She came right over and introduced herself.

"Walker tells me a lot about you," Ulsa said.

"I hope it was good."

"Oh, yes, he tells me about all your adventures—chasing sea lions into the ocean, climbing the sand dunes."

"Yes, well, I try to show them a good time."

"I wish we had the chance for that kind of thing. Do you ever take girls along?"

"I'm afraid not."

That was the problem, of course. Women would distract the boys from the mission at hand. Sure enough, as they sat round the fire, the boys vied for Ulsa's attention, ignoring him entirely.

"What was the best thing you saw today?" Walker wanted to know.

"We saw a rhinoceros!" Ulsa said. "It was amazing!"

"You're lucky," Elliot said. "We haven't seen one."

"Also, we saw some, how do you say, *warzenschwein*. Like a pig. With two big teeth." She held her fingers up to her mouth.

"Do you mean a warthog?" Walker said.

"Yes, warthog."

Chas snickered. "*Warzenschwien*. You Germans. *Achtung*! *Warzenschwein*!"

Paul weighed in. "So, Walker's about to undertake a risky exploration," he said.

"What's that?"

"Do you know the explorer, David Livingstone?"

"Yes, I know of him."

"Cecil heard that he carved his initials in a tree on an island in the middle of the Zambezi. He and Walker are going to wade out there tomorrow and see if they can find it. The island is right above the falls."

She looked at Walker with concern. "But this sounds dangerous."

"It could be," he said. "Cecil and I are going to check it out more carefully in the morning."

She grabbed his hand, all but throwing both arms around him. "*Aber*, Walker, no!"

Cecil had heard enough. "Yes, well, we need to be turning in. We're headed out early in the morning."

He gave Walker a hard look. The boy got to his feet and escorted dear Ulsa back to her campsite.

Chapter 12

When Walker came through the door with Mary Beth, he watched his parents' faces fall. It was her boots—the leather boots and the mini-skirt. In Mary Beth's perfectly fine middle-class world, this was standard dress. But for Walker's high-brow parents, it was a shocking display of flesh, an invitation to their son to explore the barely hidden prize.

"Mom, Dad, this is Mary Beth," he said.

Mary Beth smiled and offered her hand. His parents shook it, stone-faced.

"Can I get you something to drink?" his mother said. "A ginger ale?"

"A ginger ale would be fine."

His mother hurried off to the kitchen.

His father stood for a moment, then led the way to the wood-paneled living room. He settled into a stuffed chair while Mary Beth admired the built-in bookshelf that spanned an entire wall.

"Wow, have you read all these books, Mr. Scoville?" she said.

He gave a quick laugh. "Yes. They're not just there for looks."

Walker fumed at the insult, but Mary Beth took it in stride. She turned, smiled, and sat on the couch next to Walker. His father's eyes darted to the shadow inside her skirt.

"Let's go in the sunroom," Walker said to Mary Beth. "It's got a better view."

The Scovilles' house sat on a hill overlooking the Housatonic River. The picture window in the sunroom framed it all—the dark, swirling water fringed by a hardwood forest rising to pale green meadows. It was one of the finest views in the state.

"Oh, my gosh, this is stunning," Mary Beth said.

"Dad's always cutting the tops off of the trees so we can see the river," Walker said. "It'll kill them eventually."

His father, standing just behind, snorted. "If it was up to you, we wouldn't see anything but trees."

His mother arrived with the drinks. Mary Beth thanked her.

"I've ridden the horse trail along the river, but I've never seen it from up high," she said.

"Oh, you ride?" his mother said.

"Yes, I have an old gelding. Chance."

His father lit up. "Is he at the Hunt Club? I haven't seen you down there."

"No, I can't afford those prices. I keep him at home. We have a stable and a small pasture."

"Where is that?" his mother said.

"It's out on County Line Road. Past Dobson's Mill."

His mother seemed to consider that. Yes, Mom, it's out there among the small houses. On small acreage. With blue glass balls in the yard.

Mary Beth sat down, crossed her legs, and began bobbing her booted foot. Again, his father's eyes jumped to her midsection. Jesus, Dad.

In truth, those gorgeous legs had been the first thing Walker noticed about Mary Beth. On a rare occasion Choate played against a public school, Mark Sheehan High, in basketball. He and Schwartzy had sat together in the bleachers, checking out the girls on the other side of the court. There was one, in particular, wearing a very short mini-skirt, sitting in the first row.

As the game started, Walker stole glances at her between the onrushing players. She was following her team coming down the court when suddenly, very clearly, she fixed her gaze on him. She didn't stare, more like grazed her eyes across his. But he was hooked.

"Dude, I think this girl is checking me out!" he said to Schwartzy.

"Well, go talk to her at half-time."

"Yeah, maybe."

Half-time came. Walker got up to go to the bathroom. Then, he went to get a Coke. By the time he came back, the players had already come out of the locker room. He sat down next to Schwartzy.

"Did you talk to her?" Schwartzy said.

"No. I don't know what to say."

"Jesus, man. She's looking right at you. In fact, here she comes!"

The next thing Walker knew, she was standing in front of him.

"I'm Mary Beth," she said. "When were you planning to speak to me?"

He blushed. "I'm sorry, I just..."

"Not very brave, are you?"

He laughed. "No."

"Don't worry about it," she said. "When are you going to ask me out?"

This was one of many things he came to love about her—her boldness, her playfulness. She was comfortable around boys regardless of their woodenness and their predictability. She was a people person and showed her love easily.

Walker was slower to respond. Despite his advantages in status and education, he was unsure of himself in her presence. She was unabashed in pointing out his faults—the sprinkling of dandruff on the shoulders of his blue blazer, the prep school sarcasm that failed to impress. But she did not condemn him, and as they started dating steadily he found he craved her honesty. In her presence, he slowly blossomed, shedding the rigid formality that constrained his instincts and spontaneity.

"Talk!" she had all but barked when he grew sullen over some offense.

"What do you mean?"

"Talk. You're upset about something."

He screwed up his courage. "Your make-up. I don't like the smell of it."

"Okay, I'll change it. I've got lots of different kinds. Just let me know what you like."

She literally, physically, loosened him up, starting with his wooden dancing. A modern-day Dorothy from the Wizard of Oz, she oiled his joints one at a time.

"There you go," she said, tapping his shoulder. "Now, wave it around."

This carried over to sex. She slowed his hand when he explored her most sensitive parts, vocally expressed her pleasure. Most of the girls he'd known never even let him get that far. But sex, ultimately, marked the beginning of the end of their relationship. His parents made no secret of their disdain for Mary Beth's lack of social standing. A few dates with a girl from the other side of the tracks was one thing, but the steady affair that developed, the genuine love their son seemed to feel for this girl, was too much. Why, his father wondered, was he not interested in any of the girls that went to Rosemary Hall?

"They don't get my sense of humor," Walker said.

His father sniffed. "Sense of humor."

One night, he was making out with Mary Beth in the kitchen. His parents had gone to bed, leaving the swinging door to the kitchen closed. Walker backed Mary Beth up against the counter and pushed his groin into hers until the smell of her sex filled the room. He raised her skirt over her hips and slid his hand inside her panties. Just then, his mother came through the door.

"Walker!" she shouted. "You take her home right now! I'm calling her mother."

To Walker's surprise, Mary Beth's mom didn't banish him from seeing her. She told her daughter she hoped she was being careful about sex, which Mary Beth assured her she was. Walker's parents, meanwhile, expressed their "disgust" at his behavior and suggested it was time he ended the relationship. "Before something happens that you'd regret for the rest of your life." To their amazement, he refused to comply. He continued to see Mary Beth but was always on edge, devoid of joy.

"This isn't working," Mary Beth said to him. "Your parents are never going to approve of us."

"Fuck them," Walker said. "I don't need their approval."

The coup de grace came when his father said he would only pay for the trip to Africa if Walker would end his relationship with Mary Beth. Sitting in the car on what proved to be their final date, Walker held her hand and opened his mouth to speak.

"Listen, I..." The words stuck in his throat.

"You what?" Mary Beth said. "Speak."

"I..."

"You can't say it. I will. Let's end this relationship."

Walker wanted to cry. His eyes filled with tears, but he couldn't manage to cry. He gasped like a fish out of water, mouth opening and closing, opening and closing.

"It's okay," she said. "You're a good boy."

Chapter 13

Everyone assembled on the banks of the Zambezi to see Cecil and Walker off. Cecil carried a walking stick, and Walker a backpack with Cecil's movie camera, a flashlight, a small bag of plaster of Paris, and a tin pie plate. If they found Livingstone's inscription, Cecil wanted physical proof that he could carry back to England. A plaster cast of the man's trademark initials—a capital D overlaid by a capital L—would be that proof.

At Cecil's urging, Walker led the way, stepping through the papyrus grass into the channel that led to the first island and, hopefully, to the main channel of the Zambezi. The bottom was firm, and the water knee-deep. The current swirled around his legs with enough pressure to challenge his footing but not to sweep him off his feet.

"Looking good, guys!" Schwartzy called from the bank.

"Be careful, baas!" Patrick echoed.

If at any point either Walker or Cecil felt unsafe, they agreed they would both turn around. So far, that was not a problem. Cecil followed cautiously, planting his walking stick firmly before bringing his other foot forward. It was slow going, but step by step, they made their way across and onto the far bank.

A cheer went up.

"Nicely done!" Chas yelled. "What savages you are!"

"Watch out for snakes!" Elliot said.

Cataract Island was densely wooded—a dark tangle of vines and tree trunks rising to an unbroken canopy. Walker felt an unexpected thrill. Everywhere Cecil had taken them so far had been visited by other tourists. But this was virgin territory, trod by no one except possibly native hunters and fishermen.

He parted branches, searching the ground for game trails. There were more than a few, possibly made by baboons or warthogs. Here and there, the soil was turned up, a sign of the latter rooting for tubers. Passing between two bushes, he caught a last-second glimpse of a spider suspended in front of him and felt the web stick to his face.

"Shit!" he cried.

"What?" Cecil said. "What's happened?"

"Fucking spider bit me."

"Where?"

"Right on the face. Are any of these things poisonous?"

"I don't think so. Let me have a look."

He inspected Walker's cheek. "Doesn't look too bad. In any case, there's nothing we can do. Let's keep going."

Cecil's apparent lack of concern bothered Walker. The man was focused on only one thing—his chance at fame.

For what seemed like half an hour, they bushwhacked their way through the forest. Finally, a window of daylight appeared through the trees. Walker parted a last branch and looked out at a wide expanse of water swirling among the rocks.

"This is the main channel!" he called to Cecil. "I can see the mist coming up from the falls!"

Cecil came beside him, out of breath. He wiped a handkerchief across his brow and stared downstream.

"There it is," he said. "Do you see it? Right in the middle of the channel."

A hundred yards downstream, a wooded island stood out against the fall line. "It's a long way."

"We've come this far," Cecil said. "We can't stop now."

Walker stepped back into the river, angling downstream with the current. Each yard closer to the island was a yard closer to safety, but it was also a yard closer to the falls. Feel for the next rock, put your weight down, and test it for stability. This one's loose! Try to the left.

A cry rang out. He turned to see Cecil fallen in the river, being slowly rolled by the current. He hesitated. "Can you get up?"

Cecil planted his wading stick in the bottom, tried to stand, and fell back down.

"For God's sake, help me!"

He waded back and grabbed Cecil by the hand. Before he could get a firm footing, the man pulled him over. Walker fell face-first into the water, touched the bottom, and stood back up. "Let me get my footing!" he yelled.

He reached under Cecil's armpits. "Okay. Now."

Cecil grabbed for Walker's belt and pulled himself upright, his hot breath in Walker's face.

"Christ, that gave me a fright," Cecil said. "I thought you were going to let me drown."

"What do you mean?"

"You just stood there."

"No, I didn't!"

Cecil seemed surprised by Walker's emotion. He looked downstream.

"Do you want to turn back?" Walker said.

"No, we're almost there. Just don't leave me."

They waded the last hundred feet arm in arm, collapsing together as they reached solid ground. Walker immediately shed his backpack to inspect its contents. He felt the camera, the paper bag of plaster.

"Is it ruined?" Cecil said.

"It's damp, but it's not soaked. I think everything's alright."

"Thank God."

Walker stood up and inspected the shoreline. There was a faint trail leading into the bush. People had been here before.

Cecil rose and steadied himself. "Alright. Carry on."

They started along the trail, scanning the forest for a baobab tree. The roar of the falling water and the mist in the air signaled their approach to the edge. Through the broken canopy, Walker spotted a smooth, gray trunk topped by a sparse array of branches. It was definitely a baobab. And it was old.

"Here's one!" he said.

Cecil brushed past him and began to circle the tree.

"It's got a cavity," he said. "Quick, hand me the torch."

Walker dug the flashlight out of the pack and handed it over.

Cecil crouched inside the tree. "It's ginormous!"

Walker stuck his head behind, inhaling the dank smell.

"There's something here," Cecil said.

His beam illuminated a set of initials.

"TN," Walker said.

"No, that's clearly not it," Cecil said.

He moved the beam around, pausing on another inscription. There it was—a D overlaid by an L. "This is it!" he cried.

"Are you sure?"

"Absolutely. I've seen others like it."

Cecil backed out of the cavity. "It's too dark to film. We'll have to rely on the casting. Get the pan and the plaster. Go down to the river, put the plaster in the pan, and sprinkle in some water."

"How much do I add?"

"Until it feels like putty. Use a stick to mix it."

Walker gathered the materials and followed the path toward the end of the island, toward the deafening roar of Victoria Falls. He stepped into the sunlight and confronted a veil of mist—a portal to another world. Not thirty feet away, the Zambezi tumbled into the abyss.

He found a stick among the rocks and knelt by the pool. He poured the plaster into the pan, cupped water by hand from the river, and mixed it to the consistency of dough. He brought the pan back and set it at Cecil's feet.

"Brilliant," Cecil said.

Cecil leaned into the cavity. "I'll have to hold it in place for a good fifteen minutes. I'm not sure I can do it that long."

"We can trade off. Just let me know when you get tired."

Cecil raised the plate and slapped it against the trunk. He checked his watch.

"3:15. Now, we wait."

The minutes passed. Walker crouched outside, looking over Cecil's shoulder.

"So, when was Livingstone here?"

"1854. He was researching trade routes to the Indian Ocean. He was the first European to cross Central Africa."

"I hear he was one of the first to call for the end of the slave trade, too."

"Yes, well..."

They crouched for a time in silence, the roar of the falls filling the air.

"My arm is cramping," Cecil said. "Can you take over?"

Cecil's hand brushing against Walker's as they traded places. Walker held the plate against the trunk.

"What are you going to do with this thing if it comes out?" Walker asked.

"I shall take it back to London and present it to the Royal Geographic Society."

"And what will they do for you?"

"They should give me some respect. You, as well."

Walker pondered that. Now, his arm was growing tired. "How much longer?" he said.

"That should be enough time. Let's see what we've got."

Walker took the pressure off, and the cast fell into his hands. It was speckled with pieces of rotten wood, but underneath was a clear impression of the man's signature. He handed it to Cecil, who carried it out into the daylight.

"It's magnificent," Cecil said. "Absolutely magnificent!"

As Walker emerged from the cavity, Cecil leaned forward, took his face in hand and kissed him square on the lips. Walker pulled away and wiped his hand across his mouth.

"Sorry," Cecil said. "I got a bit carried away. Are you alright?"

He was not. The man who seconds ago was his hero

now appeared as a monster. The adventure that was to be a testimony to his budding manhood was ending in shame. He shouldered the pack and made his way back toward the river.

※

By the time Walker and Cecil made it to camp, the sun had set and the boys had a fire going. Seeing the two men approaching, they jumped to their feet.

"Did you find it?" Elliot called.

They gathered around as Cecil reached into the pack and held up the casting like an Olympic medal.

"Son of a bitch, you found it!" Schwartzy said. "He slapped Walker on the back. "So, you're his golden boy now!"

Walker brushed past and sat on his cot while the others celebrated. Schwartzy followed him.

"What's up, dude?" he said.

"I'll tell you about it later."

Ulsa saw the commotion and came over to inquire what was going on.

"Cecil and Walker discovered the Holy Grail," Chas said. "David Livingstone's initials."

Cecil presented her with the plaster cast. And Walker saved the day, I might add. I fell in the river and would have drowned if not for him."

"He saved you?" she said.

"Quite literally."

Walker met Cecil's eye. The man was trying to build him up in front of Ulsa. He appreciated that, but when Ulsa came over and hugged him, he barely found the strength to respond.

"You're a hero!" she said. "You're going to be famous."

"It wasn't me who made the discovery," he said.

"But you were part of it!"

She snuggled up next to him on the cot. He was the envy of all the boys, and yet he felt like a fraud, a weakling. Meanwhile, Cecil reveled in replaying the details of their expedition. He seemed drunk, dancing and singing in front of the fire. "We're marching to Pretoria, Pretoria, Pretoria…"

"What's wrong?" Ulsa said. "You're not talking."

"I'm really tired."

"Something's happened. Tell me."

Tears started in his eyes.

"What?" she said.

He was about to speak when a pair of headlights swung into the campground, blinding him and Ulsa. He held up his hands to block the light, made out the silhouette of a police car. The passenger side door opened, and out stepped a tall boy dressed in shorts and a T-shirt. He walked into the firelight, a sick smile on his face. Alec.

Chapter 14

Cecil stared in disbelief as Alec walked up with his hand extended in greeting. He stormed past the boy to confront the two police officers who'd just stepped out of the car.

"What's the meaning of this?" Cecil demanded.

"Calm down, sir," the chief officer said. "Are you Cecil Covington?"

"I am."

"Let's have a seat in the car."

While the other officer kept an eye on Alec, Cecil got into the car. The first officer explained that Alec had been arrested in Windhoek two days earlier for soliciting a prostitute.

"Oh, good lord!"

"He claimed to be an American citizen on safari. They asked him what outfit he was with, and he gave them your name. He said you'd left him behind and were headed up this way."

Cecil scoffed. "I didn't leave him behind; I sent him home for gross misbehavior. He was supposed to fly back to the States. I paid for his ticket!"

"He had quite a bit of cash on him. He also had this."

The officer reached into his glove compartment and produced a large pistol. "Do you know anything about this?"

"I most certainly do not. He must have bought it in Windhoek."

"He's allowed to own one, but he has to have a license to carry it."

"He won't touch it again until he's on his way home. I'll pack it away."

The officer gave him the gun. "What exactly did he do to get himself tossed off your trip?"

"He threw rocks at a lion in Etosha."

"Yerra! Good Christ!"

"Then, he pissed on a pangolin."

"Pissed on a pangolin. What the bloody hell for?"

"Just for the hell of it, I suppose. He's one of these bastards who's mad at the world. Wish I'd known that when I recruited him."

The officer looked out the window at the boys, gathered now around the fire. "Who are these chaps anyway? They all from the States?"

"All except the African. He's from Windhoek. I hired him as a driver to take Alec's place. Cost me a fortune."

"You're an outfitter, are you?"

"A filmmaker. Wildlife. I bring the boys along to help pay my way."

"Good money in wildlife films?"

Cecil sighed. "If you can get it on the telly. But there's a lot of competition these days. You have to have something quite exceptional."

"I heard they spotted a giant sable antelope up on the Kavango River. That's a rare animal, ja?"

Cecil came alert. "Someone saw a giant sable antelope? When?"

"A few days ago. It was in the paper. SADF spotted him while they were out on patrol."

"Oh, my goodness. Do you know there's never been one filmed in the wild? Tell me what paper this was in. What was the date?"

"It was in yesterday's *Herald*."

"I must find a copy."

The officer produced a clipboard and a pen. "I need you to sign off on this form. This says you've taken responsibility for your Alec."

Cecil signed the form. The officer took it back and put it on the dash. He nodded at the gun in Cecil's hand.

"Make sure he packs that away, or he could be arrested again."

"Alright. Thank you for bringing him along, I suppose. Don't know what I'm going to do with him."

"Good luck."

Cecil got out of the car and stomped over to the red Land Rover. All eyes were on him as he threw the pistol in the back. He slammed the tailgate and walked over to confront Alec.

"You've no doubt told the others, but why don't you explain to me why you didn't go home," he said.

Alec shrugged. "Didn't want to."

"What were you planning to do? Spend the rest of your days whoring around Windhoek? You've already cost me a fortune. I've had to hire a driver to take your place."

"I can still drive," Alec said.

"You most certainly will not."

Cecil turned to Patrick. "This boy is not to take the

wheel under any circumstance. Do you understand?"

"Yes, baas."

Cecil turned to Alec. "I've given Patrick your cot, so you'll have to sleep on the ground for the rest of the trip. There's an extra sleeping bag in the back of my car."

"Suits me."

"I'm turning in. I don't want to be bothered. By any of you!"

In the morning, Cecil decided he would go to The Victoria Falls Hotel for breakfast and possibly lunch. He needed to get away from these boys, Alec, for certain, and Paul and Walker, as well. Both of them were giving him the hairy eyeball. He could well imagine why. Walker seemed to share everything with Paul.

Cecil rummaged through his duffle bag to find a clean set of clothes and managed to come up with a rumpled pair of khakis and a slightly stained button-down shirt. His sole pair of plimsolls were still damp from yesterday's river crossing, but they would have to do. He changed clothes behind the vehicle and appeared in front of the group.

"I'm off to breakfast at The Victoria Falls Hotel," he said. "You all are free to do what you like. Perhaps Patrick can drive you into town."

"Are you going to make us breakfast first?" Elliot asked.

"Make it yourself. You should have learned by now."

He got behind the wheel and sped out of the campground. His rage dissipated as he entered the lovely town. In minutes, he was passing beneath the shady jacarandas and through the archway that bore the hotel's name. The Victoria had stood the test of time, unlike so much else in this country. Built in 1904, its red tile roof and stucco siding gleamed in the morning sun. The colonnaded porch was empty at this hour, but the high-backed chairs would soon be occupied. By the right kind of people, mind you.

Cecil parked his car and strode into the high-ceilinged lobby. The male receptionist frowned at his approach.

"Oh, dear," Cecil said. "I'm afraid I'm not properly dressed."

"How may I help you, sir?"

"I'm here for breakfast."

"May I suggest the back porch? Lovely view."

"Yes, fine. Listen, I'm eager to get a copy of yesterday's *Herald*. Might you have one lying around?"

"I'm afraid we toss the paper out at the end of the day."

"Yes, but I must find a copy. There's an article in there I want to read."

The receptionist sighed. "Well, if you *must*, you may be able to find a copy in the rubbish. That would be out back. Through the doorway to your right."

"Lovely, thanks."

Cecil went out the back door and scanned the environs. Here was a collection of broken chairs, a rusted lawn mower, and a large metal container that reeked of rotten food. He stood on tiptoes to see over the edge. The container was filled with stained boxes, crumpled paper napkins, and leftovers from last night's dinner. Amidst this mess, he spied the corner of a newspaper. He looked around to see if anyone was watching, then hoisted himself over the edge. Landing atop the pile, he knelt and recovered the paper.

He was scanning the masthead to confirm the date when a hail of garbage rained down on his head. He looked up to see dark-skinned hands holding a waste basket.

"You idiot!" he yelled.

A nappy-haired face peered over the edge. "I'm so sorry, sir. I didn't see you."

"Are you blind?"

"No, sir. But what are you doing in there?"

"I was looking for yesterday's paper. Now, help me out."

Cecil struggled to his feet and brushed the garbage out of his hair.

"How do I look?"

"Fine, sir."

"Lovely. Thanks for your help."

He went back inside, holding up the folded newspaper and smiling at the receptionist. He strolled through the lounge, where an elderly White woman waved her nose as he passed. He arrived at the back terrace with its famous view of the Zambezi River and the railway trestle spanning the gorge. He took a seat at a table and waved to the African waiter.

"Might I have a fried egg and some sausage?" Cecil said.

"Yes, sir."

"And I'll have some tea. A bit of lemon."

"Yes, sir."

The waiter left. He unfolded *The Herald*. TWO POLICE DEAD IN SWA BLAST, the headline blared. Phooey on that. He flipped to the second page and the third. There it was— *RARE ANTELOPE SPOTTED ON KAVANGO RIVER. Police on patrol near the town of Mbane in South West Africa spotted what they claim was a giant sable antelope grazing on the Angolan side of the Kavango River. The giant sable is an extremely rare subspecies of the more common sable antelope. It is found only in Angola, primarily in the dense forests in the central part of that country. Wildlife biologists suspect that civil war in the newly independent nation may have driven the animal out of its traditional range.*

Blast, if he'd only learned about this when they were up in the Etosha Park. He would have gone straight there.

The waiter arrived with his breakfast.

"Lovely, thanks."

Cecil flipped back to the front page and its disturbing headline about the killing of the policemen in the Caprivi Strip. Their vehicle had hit a mine in the road, killing the two officers aboard. Officials suspected that the mine had been planted by members of PLAN operating out of Angola. In response, the government called on SADF to help defend the area. Christ, these rebels were becoming a real nuisance!

The terrace began to fill with other patrons—a bunch of overweight, elderly White tourists in identical, freshly-ironed safari outfits. No doubt they thought of themselves as quite adventurous. Took a sunrise cruise on the Upper Zambezi, did you? Spotted a bloat of hippos? Then, again, that could be him in not too many years. He'd just turned sixty and surely wouldn't be doing this much past sixty-five. And what would he be then—a has-been tour leader, alone—an outcast?

He finished his breakfast and pushed the plate aside. The waiter arrived and asked if he wanted anything else. No, he did not. He paid the bill and walked back through the hotel, passing beneath the mounted heads of lion and buffalo. Magnificent specimens, these! He read the plaques—*Shot by Yank Allen, July 1901. Shot by William Charles*

Baldwin, August 1865. These big game hunters had left their mark for the ages, but what mark would he leave for all his years in Africa? There was his discovery of Livingstone's initials, or perhaps the rediscovery. Someone at the Geographic Society was bound to say so-and-so saw them in such-and-such year. But he was quite certain no one had filmed a giant sable antelope. Not alive, and not in the wild. This would be his mark!

He strode up to the receptionist. "Might you have a road atlas handy? I've left mine in the car."

"Indeed we do," the receptionist said. "I keep one handy for those who need a little help finding their way around."

"Quite."

The man reached under the counter and pulled out a tattered atlas of Southern Africa.

"Marvelous. I'll return it in a jiffy."

He carried the atlas out to the veranda and found a chair next to a silver-haired gentleman in a tweed jacket. The man stared at his muddy shoes. Yes, well, see what you look like after wading the Zambezi!

He flipped through the pages to the map of South West Africa. Where was this town of Mbane? He ran his finger along the narrow protrusion at the northeast corner of the country—the Caprivi Strip. Here it was on the Kavango River, just across the border from Angola. Christ, it was a long drive—hundreds of kilometers. What were the chances he could get past these silly roadblocks? And what was the chance this lone giant sable was still around? But this was what real exploration was about. This was what *he*, Cecil Covington, was about.

Chapter 15

Patrick and the boys managed to cram into the blue Land Rover for the short trip downtown. They were understandably subdued with Alec back in their midst and Cecil gone off on his own. Patrick didn't know exactly what Alec had done, but he knew it must be serious for Cecil to have ordered him home. It made him nervous to have this boy in the front seat.

They hadn't gone far when Alec spoke to him. "So, Cecil hired you to take my place, huh?"

"He has hired me to drive this vehicle, yes."

His nervousness must have shown, for Alec responded, "Don't worry about it."

"Wow, that's big of you, Alec," Chas said.

Alec gave Chas the finger.

What a mess this was. Patrick partly wished he'd stayed home in Windhoek, but if he was ever to run his own tour guide business, he had to learn to get along with a variety of people.

They entered downtown and crossed the tracks by the train station. A train had just arrived, the steam engine parked just short of the road.

"Patrick, can you pull over here?" Elliot said. "I want to get some pictures."

He found a parking space, and the boys piled out with their cameras, all except Alec, who seemed not to care about the train. He wandered about while Patrick stayed behind him, mindful of Cecil's instruction to keep a close eye on the boy.

Across the street, three soldiers—two White and one Black—sat cradling automatic weapons in an open-topped Rhodesian Army vehicle. This drew Alec's attention. He boldly approached the soldiers and asked them about their rifles.

"Are those FALs?" he said.

The soldiers nodded.

"Twenty- or thirty-round magazines?"

"Thirty," one of the Whites said. "You seem to know your weapons."

"Yeah, I've studied up on it."

The other White soldier eyed him. "Are you a Brit?"

"No, I'm from the U.S."

"A Yank, neh? We don't see many of you these days. You on safari?"

"Something like that."

Alec addressed the Black soldier. "Did you get drafted?" he asked.

"Drafted? No. I volunteered."

"Why?"

"Good pay."

Alec nodded. "So, you guys get along?"

The Black soldier glanced at his companions. "Ja, we get along."

"That's cool."

All this talk made Patrick nervous. He approached Alec and urged him to come along. One of the White soldiers interrupted.

"Who are you?" he said.

Patrick froze. Did they suspect something? That he was a rebel? "I am the driver. Come, Alec. We have much to see."

Alec saluted the soldiers, "Good hunting," he said.

Patrick found the others and urged them to head on to the shopping district. The boys wandered in and out of the Indian groceries and the general dealers. They didn't find anything worth buying.

"Come see the statue of Cecil Rhodes," Patrick said. "This is a famous man."

The statue stood atop a simulated rock, a towering mustachioed figure striding forth, hand on hip. Rhodes, he explained, had developed the area's diamond mines, built the railroads, and served as imperial prime minister of what was then known as "Cape Colony." Other tourists he'd brought here were much impressed, but this group was not. Paul called the man a "capitalist pig," which made Patrick smile. A most interesting boy!

Out of ideas for what more to do, he drove the boys back to the campsite.

※

In mid-afternoon, Cecil returned. He seemed in much better spirits than when he left. He got a map out of the car and called them to the picnic table, saying he had an important announcement.

"I've just learned something fantastic!" Cecil said.

"There's been a sighting of a giant sable antelope just here along the Kavango River."

He pointed at a spot on the map, back in Namibia along the border with Angola.

"This is an extremely rare animal," he said. "It's never been filmed in the wild. I'm proposing we go there instead of heading to Mana Pools. There's a chance we could see this animal and possibly photograph him. Wouldn't that be exciting?"

Patrick had heard about the giant sable, but never seen one. It was revered by tribes in the north, in Barotseland, the kingdom that before colonization had spanned a vast region including parts of modern-day Namibia, Angola, Botswana, and Zambia. He would love to see this animal, but it was very far away, at the end of the Caprivi Strip, in an area that was the site of recent rebel activity.

"Baas, this is very far away," he said.

"Yes, it would be a three- or four-day drive, depending on the road conditions. But we would go through some wild country. Bound to be a lot of wildlife."

The boys were silent. Patrick guessed they didn't know anything about the Caprivi Strip. Back in the colonial era, when *"Sud-Ouest Afrika"* was a German colony, the Germans arranged a trade with the British—the island of Zanzibar off the coast of Tanzania in exchange for a long, narrow strip of land that would provide the colony access to the Zambezi River, which flowed into the Indian Ocean. This, the Germans thought, could become an important trade route, but what they seemed not to know was that Victoria Falls lay downstream of this piece of land and posed a natural barrier to any boat traffic. Leo von Caprivi, the German general for whom the land was named, had never been to Africa. In the end, river trade never materialized, and the Caprivi Strip was never much inhabited by Whites. Now, it was a political no man's land, used by rebels coming south from Zambia and Angola on their way to the heart of Namibia and to South Africa. He must talk to Cecil about this.

That evening, after the boys settled into a game of cards, Patrick ushered Cecil aside.

"Baas, I am worried about this plan to drive through the Caprivi Strip. I have heard bad things about this place."

Cecil frowned. "What are you talking about?"

"The rebels, sir, from the camps in Zambia and Angola. I have read in the paper that they come across this land quite often."

"Well, they're not going to bother a bunch of tourists, are they?"

"Perhaps. But the roads are sometimes mined!"

"I've read of one or two incidents, but that's no reason to stay away entirely. I'm sure SADF has things under control."

"Sir, I think we should go to Mana Pools as planned. That's where Piet said I would be going."

Cecil became angry. "I hired you to be my driver for the next two weeks. I didn't promise where we'd travel, I only suggested it. Now, we're going to the Kavango, and we're going via Caprivi."

Now, it was Patrick's turn to be angry. He went off to the blue Land Rover, sat in the front seat, and closed the door. How he wished he had his own guide service so that he could dictate the terms. More than that, even if he was just someone's driver, he deserved respect. He deserved to be listened to. This Cecil Covington was like so many other

Whites. He was pleasant to the Africans until it came to a disagreement of desires or opinions. Then, the Africans were to submit. Patrick was no one.

Perhaps Josiah had it right. There would be no respecting the Africans until the White minority governments were overthrown, until their power was taken away. They would not give it up voluntarily, only by force.

Chapter 16

The camp stood south of Lubango, a handsome town nestled into the hillside of Angola's Huila Plateau. This was the principal training camp for PLAN combatants, a formidable complex of barracks, mess hall, and headquarters around a parade ground. Upon arrival, Josiah was issued a blanket and a uniform and assigned to Barracks 3, Bed 5. He entered to find two dozen soldiers staring at him, some hostile, some unreadable. Only one gave a hint of a smile.

Emmanuel, his nearest bedmate, was also from Windhoek. He was city-born and -bred, aspiring to earn a college degree, but prohibited by apartheid.

"I am glad to meet you, my broer," Emmanuel said. "I was beginning to feel I had made a mistake volunteering for this army. These other country boys. Half the time, I don't know what they're saying."

Most of the soldiers, Josiah learned, were, indeed, country boys with calloused hands and rough manners. They had spent their lives herding cattle and hoeing fields. Some were volunteers, but others had been recruited, and some were criminals.

Emmanuel was a former postal worker. He, like Josiah,

was fed up with mistreatment at the hands of White bosses. He dreamed of an independent Namibia governed by majority rule, with opportunities for all. Mostly, he wanted a better life for his children, whom he'd left behind with his wife in Katutura.

"You have children?" Josiah asked.

"Yes. Two boys."

"You have sacrificed much to be here!"

"Yes, I've only been here a week, and I miss them already."

But as Josiah learned, there was little time for moping. At six every morning, the commandant blew his whistle. Soldiers ate a hurried breakfast of mealie pap porridge, then mustered on the parade ground for the first of several drills, beginning with a five-mile run. Josiah had played soccer in school and had run as fast as most of the boys. But that was years ago, and he had, in fact, never run five miles in his life, certainly not through heavy sand. By the third mile, he was in tears, lagging behind the group and whipped from behind by the drill sergeant.

Back at camp, he was comforted by Emmanuel. "You will catch up. Believe me," he said. "It takes a week to get your breath, neh!"

The run was followed by marching, endless marching back and forth across the parade ground. What was the purpose of this? Were they going to march in formation against SADF? Adding insult to injury, they were issued fake rifles—crude wooden replicas such as you would give a child. You couldn't shoot them, couldn't damage them. But the penalties for misusing them were harsh. Drop your gun on the ground? Do thirty push-ups. Aim it at another soldier? A day in the brig.

Afternoons were devoted to political lessons—something more to Josiah's liking. They learned of Germany's colonization of the land of the Herero and Namaqua in the 1880s under the name of German *Südwestafrika*. In 1905, the Germans formally confiscated Native land, killing or starving those who resisted. Following Germany's defeat in World War I, the Allies gave South Africa a mandate to govern South West Africa "until such time as it was prepared for self-determination." But that time never came. Instead, South Africa extended its hated policy of apartheid to its neighbor.

Africans did not take this lying down. In the 1950s, Herero students, teachers, and intelligentsia joined with Ovambo laborers to form the South West African People's Organization. SWAPO demanded immediate independence under Black majority rule. They promised universal suffrage, sweeping welfare reforms, free healthcare, free public education, nationalization of industry, and redistribution of foreign-owned land. To no avail.

In 1971, Ovambo miners and farmers staged a nationwide strike demanding an end to contract labor and the right to apply for a job based on one's skills. South Africa's response was to declare a state of emergency and put down the strike.

"And so, we are left with no choice," the political trainer said. "We must win back our country through the barrel of a gun. That is why you are here."

SWAPO's dreams of a truly democratic Namibia, governed by the Black majority, where Africans owned their own land and businesses, free of domination and humiliation by Whites, comforted Josiah at night. He wished Patrick would join him in this fight. Maybe in time, his brother would feel the same urgency for change that he did.

After two weeks, the recruits finally began combat training. The instructors taught them to crawl, not on all fours, but hugging the ground like a caterpillar. Crawl with one elbow pulling your weight forward, the opposite foot pushing from behind. After a few days, Josiah's elbows ruptured and bled. He came to hate the smell of the earth, the very soil for which they fought. But that won him no sympathy.

"Crawl, comrade. Crawl!" yelled the drill sergeant.

Crawling wasn't the worst of it. Jigger fleas emerged from the soil and bedding, burrowing between his toes and fingernails, causing constant torment and pain. Females laid their eggs in his skin, which hatched into devilish larvae. Nature, it seemed, had turned against him.

All of this changed the day they were issued AK-47 rifles, care of the Soviet Union. That country was backing rebel movements all over the frontline states of southern Africa—in the newly independent Angola, Namibia, Mozambique, Rhodesia, and South Africa. Josiah wasn't convinced that communism was the best form of government for his country, but he gladly accepted the AK-47. With these weapons, he could see the power, feel the power, hear the power. *Bam! Bam! Bam!* The watermelons used as targets flew apart on impact. Next would be the White man's head.

Finally, the day arrived when they were to go on their first mission. Josiah and Emmanuel were transferred to a small bush camp close to the Namibian border. Josiah was to head a squad of four, including Emmanuel, Johannes, and Petrus. They were to cross the Kavango into Namibia and plant a mine on the road paralleling the river. There was a chance a civilian vehicle might hit it, but most of the vehicles traveling this road were SADF patrols.

They were driven to the river at midnight, coming down out of the hills to the wooded floodplain bordering the river. The driver uncovered a dugout canoe in the brush, which they carried to the banks. He pointed just upstream to a slide mark in the mud.

"Crocodile," he whispered. "Very big."

"What if he sees us?" Josiah said.

"Paddle quickly."

The canoe was of a type made by the local Hambukushu, a Barotse tribe, carved out of a tree trunk. The four of them had no training in paddling such a craft, and they briefly argued about who should sit where. Josiah claimed the stern and told Emmanuel to sit in front of him, cradling the heavy mine.

"I'll take the front seat," Johannes said.

Petrus shook his head. "No, I should be there. I am the lightest."

"Shut up!" Josiah hissed. "Johannes, get in front. Petrus behind. Move!"

They set out onto the river, practically tipping over as soon as they reached deep water. It was a moonless night, all the better to hide their crossing from SADF patrols, but that also meant Josiah could not see any distance. Was that a crocodile coming at them? No, a tree trunk wedged in the bottom. Was that the far shore or just his imagination?

Finally, they arrived, pitching on top of each other as they slammed into the muddy bank.

Josiah winced. "Be careful! You will set off the land mine!"

They dragged the canoe into the brush and covered it with makalani palm branches. Josiah found a plastic bottle lying on the shore and wedged it into the branch of a nearby tree.

"This is our marker," he said. "The canoe will be just here."

They started off with Josiah in the lead, holding his AK-47 in the ready position. He worked his way left and right, wherever he could find an opening in the bush. The road should have been straight ahead, no more than a few hundred meters away. But after half an hour, they still hadn't found it. He called the squad to a halt.

"You have gone too far to the right!" Johannes said.

"No, we have gone left!" Petrus answered.

Josiah wiped the sweat from his face. The sky was already growing lighter. "Alright, let's fan out ten meters apart," he said. "If you strike the road, give a low '*crooo*' Like a dove."

In front of him, a clump of trees appeared to change shape. What was that? A trunk went up in the air. Elephants! A family of them!

The big bull caught his scent, and in an instant, he charged, ears flared wide, dust flying off his body. Josiah had been instructed never to fire his weapon unless he was in extreme danger, and this was it. *Bam! Bam! Bam!* He fired at point-blank range. The elephant stumbled and fell, his massive tusks plowing through the dirt just short of Josiah's boots.

Now, the cow charged, going after Emmanuel. Cradling the mine, Emmanuel had no time to shoulder his weapon. The elephant gored him and drove him to the ground.

Josiah yelled, "Fire! Fire!"

All three rifles opened up. The cow fell to her knees and rolled slowly to one side.

It wasn't until she lay inert that the men stopped firing. The younger elephants were turning in frantic circles, trumpeting in alarm. But they stayed at a distance.

Josiah dropped his weapon and ran to his friend. "Emmanuel, are you hurt? Speak to me!"

Deep, drawn-out moans rose from Emmanuel's grimaced face. Blood poured from a massive wound in his abdomen.

Johannes came beside him. "He's finished," he said.

Josiah shook his head. "No, he's only wounded. I will carry him."

Josiah lifted Emmanuel onto his back.

"Take hold," he said to his friend.

Emmanuel managed a weak grip around his neck. Petrus and Johannes shouldered the guns. They left the mine. Together they walked, step by labored step, through the bush, back to the river. He could feel Emmanuel's blood soaking through into his uniform, his faint breath against his neck.

"Hold on, my friend," he cried.

They found the canoe and dragged it to the river's edge. Josiah lay Emmanuel in the stern, jumped in, and pushed off.

"Go!" he cried to the others. "Hard!"

As they reached midstream, the sun rose over the trees and threw a golden light across the water. It was as beautiful a sight as he'd ever seen, yet right before him, his friend lay dying, his bright red blood filling the hull.

Emmanuel stared. "Josiah?"

"I'm here."

"Tell my wife I love her. Tell my children."

"Yes, I will. But we are almost there. We're almost across."

"Tell them..."

The canoe rode up on the muddy shore. Emmanuel's head rolled to one side and lay still.

Chapter 17

In the confusion that followed Alec's arrival at camp at Victoria Falls, Walker abandoned any attempt to explain to Ulsa the distress he was feeling about Cecil's kiss. She sensed that she was not wanted and left in tears. Walker was sick about it. He needed to talk to someone. It wasn't until the next day, during the trip to town, that he unburdened himself to Schwartzy.

"He kissed you?" Schwartzy said. "On the lips?"

"Yes."

"What did he say when you pulled away?"

"He apologized. He said he got carried away with all the excitement."

"Maybe that's all there was to it."

"I don't know. I think the whole thing might have been a setup. A chance for him to get me alone."

"No, I don't think so. He trusts you, man. That's why he wanted you along."

Walker was silent for a time. "Do you think I'm a wimp?"

"A wimp? No, you're not a wimp."

"Why did he pick me?"

Schwartzy patted him on the back. "Face it, man, you're pretty good-looking. He sure as hell wouldn't have wanted to kiss me."

Walker managed a smile. "How am I supposed to act around him now?"

"Just be cool. If he doesn't do it again, then chalk it up to experience. He's the one who should feel bad about it."

"Okay. But don't tell anyone else."

"I won't. And don't let it spoil Africa for you."

Those last words settled Walker down enough to let him sleep that night. Meanwhile, there were other issues at play. Everyone was concerned about how Alec would fit back into the group. And now Cecil had come up with this idea of finding this giant sable antelope, taking the group back to South West Africa instead of going further into Rhodesia and its famed Mana Pools National Park. Cecil had boasted about Mana Pools as the country's premier destination for wildlife. Walker had particularly hoped to see a leopard and a rhinoceros, the last two remaining members of the Big Five African animals he had yet to photograph. Patrick seemed to have other concerns. As he drove out of Vic Falls with Alec, Walker, and Schwartzy, Patrick's silence was palpable.

"Patrick, are you disappointed we aren't going to Mana Pools?" Walker said.

"Yes, I like Mana Pools. There are many elephants there."

"But we'll see some where we're going, right?"

"Perhaps. I don't know this part of Namibia."

"You call it Namibia now?" Schwartzy said.

"That is what the UN has declared. Resolution 435."

"That's cool. Namibia. But don't expect Cecil to go along with it."

Patrick smiled. "No, some people don't like the change."

"Is it a long way to this place where that sable antelope was spotted?" Walker asked.

"It's very, very far. I don't know if we can get there."

"Why, because the roads are so bad?"

"Yes. And some of them may be closed."

"Who would close them?"

"The police. SADF."

"The South African Defense Force is in Namibia?"

"In the Caprivi Strip, yes. They have come recently to help the police."

Walker and Paul exchanged looks. "Why do the police need help?" Walker said.

"There has been some trouble. A mine was placed in the road. Some police were killed."

"Whoa, when did this happen?"

"I read about it a few days ago. You didn't see the newspaper in Vic Falls?"

"I haven't seen a newspaper since we left Cape Town."

Alec perked up in the front seat. "I read some stuff while I was in Windhoek," he said. "There was an article about Namibian rebels setting up bases in Angola. They're free to do that now that the Portuguese military has left."

"Maybe they'll finally kick the racist leadership out of Namibia," Schwartzy said.

Walker waited for Patrick to respond, but he was silent.

They entered an area populated by dark green, flat-topped acacia trees scattered among the tall yellow grass. Patrick kept looking sideways out the window. Suddenly, he slowed down.

"Here is a leopard!" he said.

Fifty yards off the road, in the crotch of an acacia, a

spotted form stretched out on a branch. Walker aimed his camera out the window and turned the focus ring on his telephoto lens. Like water running down a slide, the leopard slipped down the tree and disappeared into the grass.

"Shit! I missed him," he said.

"He's gone," Alec said.

Up ahead, Cecil pulled over. "Okay, Cecil has seen us," Patrick said. "Let me try something."

He put the Rover into four-wheel drive and steered into the tall grass.

"Have your camera ready."

They were just approaching the acacia when the leopard stuck his head up from the grass. Walker aimed, focused, and pressed the shutter. One shot, and the leopard disappeared.

"I got him!" he said.

Patrick smiled. "You snapped him with your camera?"

"Yes! Cecil can't doubt me now!"

"That's four of the Big Five, right, man?" Schwartzy said.

"Yes. Only the rhino to go."

They pulled back on the road and drew abreast of Cecil's car.

"We saw a leopard!" Walker said. "I got a picture."

Cecil's glanced in his rearview mirror. "Really? I'm surprised I didn't see him."

"He was in one of those acacia trees," Schwartzy said. "Patrick spotted him."

Cecil frowned. "Well, let's keep going."

They drove on through the thinly forested terrain. Here and there, fires burned in the underbrush, a smell like burnt cork filling the air.

"What's with the fires?" Alec asked. "Did people set them?"

"No, they are natural," Patrick said.

"You mean nobody's minding them? Won't they burn the whole forest down?"

"They just burn these vines and bushes. New grass will grow from the ash. It's good for the land."

Alec shook his head. "Crazy."

In the afternoon, Cecil came to a halt at a fork in the road. There were no signs indicating which way to go. To one side, a small adobe house stood beneath a meager thorn tree. Half-a-dozen barefoot children dressed in dirty hand-me-down clothes peered at the cars. From this impoverished setting, two women appeared wearing spotless, brightly colored dresses and anvil-shaped hats. Cecil beckoned them over and asked for directions. As the women pointed one way and another, Walker wondered at their situation in life. They appeared to have nothing in the way of worldly goods—no washing machines, no indoor plumbing, no electricity—yet they were clearly proud of their dress and, no doubt, worked hard to maintain it. How different were they in their desires from his own mother back home in Connecticut, leafing through the pages of *Fashion* magazine?

At length, one of the women pointed to the right. Cecil thanked her and started down the road. Walker waved and smiled at the women. They waved back.

In the late afternoon, they reached the Chobe River. Cecil pulled to a halt in front of a pontoon bridge. On the far side lay Namibia, more specifically, the Caprivi Strip. He signaled for Patrick to pull abreast.

"I've decided to stop on this side for the night," he

said. "I saw a track, back at the curve, that might get us to a nice camping spot along the river. Follow me."

Cecil drove back to the track and followed it along a bluff overlooking the river. He stopped and stepped out to study the terrain. A lovely woodland of mopane, kiaat, and Zambezi teak trees sloped down to the river bordered by papyrus and cattails. All manner of birds—cormorant, fish eagle, and yellow-billed stork—perched in the trees overlooking the water. A gray hornbill flew from a thorn tree.

"This should do nicely," Cecil said.

Walker unloaded his gear, all the while casting an eye toward the river. This was a gamey-looking spot. Rather than waiting for the group, he felt like going out alone.

"Do you mind if I go down to the river?" he said to Cecil.

"You don't want to wait for the rest of us?"

"I'm not going to go far."

"Be very careful. There's liable to be some crocodiles along the banks."

Walker worked his way down the sandy slope beneath the scattered trees. Reaching the river bank, he came upon a well-used game trail. Piles of elephant dung spotted the trail and in between the oval tracks, as large and smooth as a pie plate.

He stared across the hundred-yard-wide river. Upstream, against the far shore, he made out a series of brown humps half submerged in the water. What could those be? He peered through his telephoto. The humps sprouted nostrils, eyes, and ears. Hippos! Eight or ten of them! His heart raced. Should he run back and tell the others? No. He'd vowed to go out alone, and this was his reward.

He followed the game trail along the bank until he

was directly across from the pod. It appeared to be a family unit with both large and small animals. Could they see him? He didn't know, but they seemed undisturbed. He took a few shots and settled down to watch. The nature films he'd seen featured hippo bulls engaged in mortal combat, massive jaws agape. But these animals were happy just to sit. Most animals were happy just to sit.

Ten minutes passed without any movement. He lowered his camera and leaned back on his elbows. The sun warmed his face. It was good to be alone. All the hours on the road, in camp, and touring the parks were spent with other people. Any time they saw something worth photographing, the boys would jostle for position. It was obscene in a way. Each of them thought his photograph was exceptional, yet they were probably close to identical. Here, alone on the river bank, he had a chance at something he could call his own.

As if on cue, a malachite kingfisher landed on a reed before him. It was the most beautiful bird he'd ever seen—fiery red beak, blue-green forehead, copper breast. He was sure it would flee if he moved, so he forced himself to be still. The bird spotted something in the river, flew out, hovered, and dove. It returned to the same reed—the exact same reed—with a minnow in his mouth. What a shot this would make! In the slowest motion he could muster, Walker raised his camera and turned the focus ring. The kingfisher came into view, rising and falling on the wind. Wait for it. Wait for it. The wind died and the bobbing slowed. He pressed the shutter. Got it!

As he climbed back up the hill, he heard Schwartzy's voice ring out. "See anything?"

Schwartzy sat atop the biggest mopane tree, a good

forty feet in the air. How he got there Walker couldn't imagine. The branches were few and the drop potentially deadly. But that was Schwartzy.

"I saw a beautiful kingfisher," Walker said. "Some hippos, too."

"Hippos! Get any good shots?"

"Not really."

Elliot overheard the conversation. "You saw some hippos?"

"Yeah. They're on the other side of the river."

"I want a shot of them."

Elliot started toward the river, then stopped as he passed Walker going the opposite direction.

"You say it's not a great shot?" Elliot said.

"No, they're too far away."

Elliot sighed and followed him back to camp. Poor kid. He didn't know what to do with himself.

Evening came on, the whitewashed sands taking on a golden hue. Cecil had just fired up the stove when Patrick called from a vantage point some distance away.

"Here are some elephants!"

The boys grabbed their cameras and ran to Patrick's side. Visible between the trees, a herd of elephants approached the far side of the river. There were a dozen adults, including a bull with massive tusks, and half as many calves. One by one, they skidded down the bank and waded knee-deep into the river. At first, they merely drank, but after a while, they began to spray water across their backs.

"They are playing," Patrick said. "Do you see how the mothers squirt the little ones?"

Cecil came over and deemed the scene worthy of filming. The show went on for half an hour when the big bull decided to leave. He lumbered up the steep, yard-high bank, followed by the cows. Five of the six calves made it out, but the smallest could not manage the ascent. He made several attempts, falling back each time. A cow stood atop the bank, eyes locked on the calf.

"Shit, man, that calf's not going to make it," Schwartzy said.

At some sound, inaudible across the river, the bull turned around. He raised his trunk to eye level and waved it back and forth as if mining the air for information. He started back down the bank and, after assessing the situation, slid back into the river beside the calf. He lowered his tusks beneath the calf's rear end and started pushing. Twice, the calf fell backward down the bank. On the third try, aided by the bull, the calf succeeded, reaching level ground and running to his mother with visible joy.

Patrick clapped in delight. "This is the power of family," he said. Walker wiped away tears. Here was proof that Nature was kind. He wasn't sure that it was evidence of God, but it did seem to be spiritual in some fashion, "... a personality so vast that we have never seen her features," Thoreau said.

That evening, the boys gathered fallen branches and made a fire. Cecil cooked a "special meal" consisting of sauteed ground beef, onions, and tomatoes purchased in Vic Falls. Schartzy drummed on a log. Walker played his harmonica. The moon rose over the Chobe River, a yellow orb, reflected in the swirling water.

As the group warmed their hands around the fire, Alec broke his characteristic silence.

"So, Patrick, are you going to keep working for this same company?" he asked.

"I would like to run my own guide service someday," Patrick said.

"For Africans?"

"For all people. White and Black."

"I shouldn't think that likely," Cecil said.

"Why not?" Walker said. "He's got sharp eyes, and he knows his animals. He spotted that leopard from at least a hundred yards away."

Cecil gave him a sour look.

"What would you need to run this business?" Alec asked.

"I would need my own vehicle. That's a big expense."

"What can you get a used Land Rover for, seven hundred rands?"

"At least that," Cecil said. "I would say more like a thousand. And good ones are not easy to come by."

"Maybe you could sell him one of yours?" Walker said. "You can afford a new one."

"Don't be ridiculous!"

Walker flushed with anger. A divide was forming, not just between him and Cecil but between all the boys and their leader. He wasn't happy about that, but for the first time, he'd said what he felt. And he didn't regret it.

The coals snapped in the fire. Cecil rose.

"I shan't stay up too late," he said. "We'll be entering South West tomorrow, bright and early."

The fire dwindled, and the cold came on. The moon shone like a spotlight on the camp. From down in the valley came a sound like giants laughing. *Bwaa-ha-ha. Bwaa-ha-ha.* The hippos. The hippos were laughing.

Chapter 18

Cecil awoke in an anxious mood. He'd tossed and turned all night under that bright moon. Now, he was eager to break camp, get across the river, and head on into the Caprivi Strip. He'd never been to this part of South West Africa before and had no idea what the quality of the road might be or where they might spend the night. He fired up the stove to get the water boiling, then woke the boys.

"Chop, chop. We've got a big day ahead of us."

He dropped a quarter stick of butter into the pot and set it on the stove. He followed with six eggs and stirred, all the while keeping track of the boys' progress. Alec was taking his sweet time, sitting up in his bag and staring out at the world through mussed hair. He was angry about being back with the group, but that was his tough luck. Walker, too, was slow in getting up, uncharacteristically so. He was usually the first into the "kitchen," eager to know about the plans for the day. It was possible he was still upset about the kiss, but he shouldn't be, really. He, Cecil, had meant nothing by it.

He wondered, had Walker told others about the incident? They seemed to be growing a bit hostile towards him. Paul, quite likely, knew. He and Walker were bosom buddies. Chas? Maybe. Certainly not Patrick. Elliot was too naïve, and Alec was no friend of Walker's. So, maybe just Paul...

He noticed the butter burning in the second pan. Shit, he'd forgotten to toast the bread.

"Eggs are ready," he said. "I haven't had time to do the toast. You'll have to make your own."

Chas was first in line. "No toast?"

"You know how to do it. Or you should by now."

Chas fished a piece of bread out of the bag and, after some hesitation, dropped it in the frying pan.

"When do I turn it?" he said.

"When it's ready."

What a stupid question! No doubt, this was the first time in Chas's life he'd ever had to make his own toast.

The boys gathered around, waiting for their turn at the stove.

"So, back to Namibia, Cecil?" Paul said. "When do we get to the border?"

"It's just across the bridge. And that's 'South West Africa'."

"Do we need our passports?" Elliot said.

"I should think so. Finish your eggs and wash the dishes."

Cecil started the clean up himself, then set about packing the vehicle. When all that was done, he pondered the vehicle assignments. He didn't wish to put up with Walker's moodiness, and certainly not Alec's. They could ride with Patrick.

"Elliot, Paul, and Chas, ride with me," he said. "Come, come, now. We haven't got all day."

In short order, they reached the bridge over the Chobe River. Cecil pointed out the hippos downstream, stewing in the river. They hadn't budged from the day before and probably wouldn't for another week. Blasted water pigs had kept him up all night with their grunting.

At the far end of the bridge, the road ascended to the border post, a collection of white cinderblock buildings. A gate blocked the road, and as they approached, a uniformed agent emerged.

"Morning," the agent said. "Where are you headed?"

"Mbane. Thereabouts. We're on safari."

"Mbane? May I see some identification?"

Cecil presented his British passport. The agent studied it and peered through the window at the boys.

"Long way from the normal safari route. Lost, are you?"

"We're hoping to see some game along the Kavango."

The agent handed his passport back. "You'll be alright going to Katima Mulilo, but they've got the road blocked off going west. Only open to local traffic."

"What are you talking about?"

"We've had some incidents. Rebels coming across from Angola. Mining the road and such."

"But isn't the military dealing with that?"

"Best they can. They don't want a lot of extraneous traffic."

"I see. Thank you for the information."

As they pulled away, the boys came alive.

"Road mines?" Chas said. "We're going down a road covered with mines?"

"What are we going to do if we can't get to the Kavango?" Paul said.

Cecil gave a dismissive snort. "Utter rubbish what he said. I'm sure the road is perfectly safe."

Secretly, he began to fret. The town where the antelope had been sighted was a long way west of Katima. If they were stopped from going west, there was no point in going on.

As they neared the town of Katima Mulillo, they came upon a group of African men walking along the road. They carried some rather large drums, a wooden xylophone, and other instruments. One of the men carried a decorated spear!

"Cecil, can we stop?" Paul said. "I gotta get a picture of this!"

He pulled over to the side of the road, the Blue Rover just behind. In seconds, everyone was out of the vehicles.

Paul approached the nearest man, a towering, blue-black African. "Are you guys musicians?" he said.

The man looked confused. Patrick addressed him in Silozi.

"Shangwe. Yes, these are musicians," Patrick said. "They are on their way to a wedding in Nghweze, the Black township in Katima."

"Will they play for us?" Paul asked.

"Yes, they will play."

The men set their drums on the ground and got behind them.

"Tell them to wait," Cecil said. "I need to get my camera."

He hurried back to the Rover and retrieved his Bolex and tripod. He peered through the viewfinder. "Ready!"

The drummers started playing.

Walker called out, "This is the same beat as 'Rolling and Tumbling'! That song Clapton plays."

Paul yelled. "Get your harp!"

Walker ran to the car and came back with his harmonica. He started playing in time with the drummers—

da-DAAH da-da Da Da Da; da-DAAH da-da Da Da Da. In between, Paul sang—"*I've been rollin' and tumblin', all the whole night long.*" Da-DAAH da-da Da Da Da; da-DAAH da-da Da Da Da.

Cecil panned to each of the musician's faces. They seemed to be enjoying the accompaniment. He panned to Walker. The boy was in a trance, cheeks huffing in and out, long hair falling over his face. He'd never seen this side of him.

Paul started dancing in circles, waving his hands in the air, mucking up the film in Cecil's opinion. Finally, the drums ceased. The boys cheered. They slapped hands with the Africans. Quite chummy, this lot.

Cecil folded his tripod. "Alright, let's get going," he said. "We've got a lot of ground to cover."

Back on the road, he pondered what he had just witnessed. "I didn't know Walker was such a musician," he said to Paul.

"I knew he could play, but not like that," Paul said.

Chas, in the back seat, began to sing, "*We been rollin' and tumblin', all the whole night long. Da-DAH da-da Da Da Da; da-Dah da-da Da Da Da!*"

Elliot joined in. "*When I woke up this morning, all I had was gone.*"

This went on for some time. Finally, Cecil turned round in the seat. "Will you all please shut up!"

Katima Mulillo was a sprawling settlement of single-story homes and shops on the banks of the Zambezi. Cecil was approaching the city center when he came upon a military convoy pulled to the side of the road. Here were menacing-looking Casspirs, petrol trucks, a flatbed truck carrying an armored vehicle, and another pulling a howitzer. The boys were quite thrilled with this. He was not. There must be trouble brewing.

He found a grocery store and waved for Patrick to pull in. They stepped out into the hot midday sun. Patrick approached, wearing a frown.

"Baas, have you seen these military vehicles?"

"Yes, yes, I saw them."

"I think it would not be wise to keep going."

"Don't bother me about it just now," Cecil said. "We've got shopping to do."

He roamed the aisles, picking out cans of Spam, boxes of macaroni and cheese, white bread, eggs, and jam.

"Can we get some of that powdered orange drink?" Elliot said.

"And some cereal," Chas said. "I'm sick of eggs."

"Yes, yes, just throw them in the cart."

Out in the parking lot, Cecil loaded everything into the food box and, without further comment to Patrick, got behind the wheel.

On the way out of town, they hit the dreaded roadblock. Two police vehicles were parked on either side of the road. An officer waved him to a halt.

"Where is it you're headed, sir?" the officer said.

"We're on our way to Mbane. I and the car behind me."

"May I see some identification?"

He handed the officer his driver's license.

"British, is it? Leading some sort of safari?"

"Yes. Hoping to see some game along the river."

"Not this year, you won't. This road is closed to any but local traffic."

He'd steeled himself for this. "No, but you see, I must

get at least as far as Divundu. Have you heard about the sighting of the giant sable antelope?"

The officer furrowed his brow. "Heard something about that, yes."

"Well, I'm a filmmaker, you see. I'm on assignment from the Royal Geographic Society in London to get a video if I can. This antelope has never been filmed in the wild."

"Sorry, sir. I've got orders from SADF. Nothing but local traffic along the border."

The officer handed back the license. Cecil had one more card to play.

"Listen, I've brought these boys all the way from America just to see this animal. You simply can't turn them away. Boys, show him your passports."

Elliot, Paul, and Chas reached into their pockets and handed their passports to the officer. He opened them one by one.

"All the way from the States, eh?"

"Yes, sir," they chimed.

He handed back the passports. "I suppose you can go on. But stick to the main road. No stopping for a stroll in the bush."

Cecil beamed. "Yes, thank you!"

As soon as they were on the road, Paul burst out laughing.

"You brought us all the way from America just to see the giant sable antelope?" he said. "You didn't even know about it until a few days ago!"

"On assignment from the Royal Geographic Society?" Chas echoed.

Cecil chortled. "You have to understand these aren't the brightest people in the world. They spend most of their days dozing off."

Soon enough, the cheery mood faded. The dirt road was heavily corrugated, rattling the Land Rover's carriage. The boys gripped the door handles and stared grimly through the windows. Meanwhile, the land became ever drier and more sparsely populated. When they did come to a village, it was of the most miserable sort. A thorn bush kraal surrounded circular huts made of mud and thatch. Half-naked children in the yard waved frantically to try and get them to stop.

"What do they want?" Elliot asked.

"A few shillings, if you'd give it to them," Cecil said.

"I've got some money," Elliot said. "Shall we stop? Or I could throw it out the window."

"Don't waste your time."

A woman walking along the road turned to watch them pass. She carried a clay pot on her head, wore a wrap that held a toddler on her back, and had a bare midriff bulging with child. Typical, that. But in fact, the land seemed strangely unpopulated. The Germans had starved out the local tribes back in the 1900s and herded the survivors into concentration camps. One would have expected the population to rebound by now. Perhaps these latest troubles were driving people away.

Chapter 19

The light was getting low and the road rougher as they slogged along the Caprivi Strip. Walker was growing sick of the constant vibration caused by the corrugations. By the pained looks on Alec and Elliot's faces, they felt the same way. Finally, the brake lights in the red Rover came on. A waterhole some hundred feet distant appeared through a break in the bush.

"This looks like a decent spot to camp," Cecil said to Patrick. "Pull in behind me."

The spot was far from ideal. The waterhole was ringed by broken trees—the work of elephants—and the outer fringes covered by stiff, dry grass. But no one was in the mood to complain. The boys cleared away the fallen branches and beat down the grass, then set about arranging the cots and setting up the kitchen.

When the work was done, Walker strolled down to the waterhole. The dried mud was pockmarked with footprints of warthog, antelope, and elephant. This was a gamey place. He made a circle of the waterhole, then returned to camp.

Cecil announced dinner and ladled out spoonfuls of

beef stew. As he ate, Walker kept an eye on the waterhole. Something was bound to come along.

Just as the sun dropped into the trees, a tawny head parted the grass on the far side.

"Guys, look!" he hissed. "A cheetah!"

The cat saw them but did not spook. He, or she, was eager to have a drink of that water. Such a delicate face—small and round, black bands running like teardrops from the eyes to the mouth. Deciding these two-legged creatures were not harmful, the cheetah strode into full view, trailed by three kittens.

"A mother!" Walker breathed, "How old do you think those kittens are?"

"They can't be more than a week," Cecil said.

"Shall we get our cameras?" Elliot said.

Schwartzy shook his head, "It's too dark. Just watch them."

The cheetah approached the water and then, scared off by something, backed away. The kittens shied away, too.

"Everybody be still!" Walker hissed.

Slowly, she returned to the waterhole. She went into a crouch, eyes locked on the humans across the way, and started to drink. The kittens followed suit, first one, then the others.

"This is quite remarkable!" Cecil said. "You boys are lucky to see this."

Suddenly, the surface exploded. An enormous thing—a crocodile—shot out of the water and engulfed the mother cheetah's head. It dragged the big cat into the water where it rolled once, then disappeared.

Walker jumped up. "Oh, my God! Oh, my God!"

The kittens stared at the empty space, mewing in confusion.

"Where's the cheetah?" Schwartzy yelled. "What happened!"

"Crocodile," Cecil said. "It dragged her right under!"

"She's gone? The cheetah's gone?" Elliot said.

"I'm afraid so."

Walker turned to Cecil, his face filled with anger. "A twenty-foot crocodile? In a waterhole the size of a swimming pool?"

"Quite unusual, but yes. They sit just under the surface, waiting for animals to come down to drink. Thank God it didn't grab you!"

The kittens wandered along the water's edge, searching for their mother. Their pathetic mews filled the air.

"What's going to happen to them?" Elliot said.

Cecil frowned. "If that croc doesn't get them, something else will. They won't last the night, I'm afraid."

At this, Alec stepped forward.

"Stay away from the waterhole!" Cecil said. "There could be another croc!"

Alec ignored him and strode around the bank, waving his arms at the kittens. "Get back! Get back!"

The kittens cowered at the sight of this new monster, retreating to the edge of the tall grass. Alec drove them further in.

"You're not going to save them!" Cecil yelled. "Come back. It's getting dark!"

The waterhole faded to black. Walker sat down and tried to finish his meal, but everything had changed. This place, this land that had yielded one treasure after another, had turned into a house of horrors. A full-grown cheetah—the only one they'd seen in three weeks in Africa—had been obliterated in a second. Not just any cheetah, but a mother. And now her three innocent kittens were going to die. And there was nothing he could do about it.

Where was Thoreau in this? How was this Wilderness the salvation of anything? In the early days of the trip, everything seemed dazzling and alive. Even the deserts of Namibia had a purity about them. Thoreau's insights about Nature seemed to be validated at every turn. But no crocodile had erupted from Walden Pond. No elephants had mowed down the trees along Old Marlborough Road.

As if to confirm his doubts, a hyena called out of the darkness. "*Oooh-Hoo! Oooh-hoo!*"

"Oh, dear," Cecil said.

"Does it smell the kittens?" Elliot asked.

"If it hasn't yet, it soon will."

Alec stood and shouted into the darkness. "Fuck you! Fuck you!"

"That's quite enough," Cecil said.

Alec turned. "And fuck you, too." He stormed over to the blue Land Rover, got inside, and slammed the door.

The boys exchanged glances. Alec's outburst was uncalled for. But at the same time, Walker sensed something different about him, something hopeful. The guy actually cared.

※

The next morning, the boys searched the grass around the waterhole for signs of the kittens. Nothing. What would they have done if they'd found them? There was no carrying them to safety.

After breakfast, they packed up the cars and prepared to leave. Alec got in the blue Land Rover with Patrick, but no one else made a move toward that car. Finally, Walker relented. He would deal with Alec's moodiness.

The countryside they passed through seemed abandoned. A handsome farmhouse had its windows boarded up. A tractor stood in the middle of a half-planted field. They hadn't passed a car all morning.

"Is it going to be like this the whole way across the Caprivi Strip?" Alec asked.

Patrick shook his head. "I don't know. I don't know this road."

Walker studied Alec from behind. After throwing rocks at the lions and pissing on the pangolin, it seemed out of character for him to take such pity on the cheetah. What was going on with this guy?

The question spilled out before he had time to think. "So, Alec, what happened to your father?"

Alec turned. He cupped his hands as if holding a length of pipe to his mouth. "Blaah!" He jerked his head backward.

Walker didn't understand. And then it came to him. Alec was imitating his father holding the barrel of a gun.

"Your father committed suicide?"

"Yup."

"How long ago was that?"

"Ten years."

"So, you were, like, eight years old?"

"Yup."

Walker sank back in the seat. Now, it all made sense. Alec was angry. At his father for having abandoned him. At the world for being the world ...

"Have you talked to a therapist?"

"Nope."

Walker nodded. "Sorry for bringing it up. It's none of my business."

"It's okay," Alec said. "You're the first one I've talked to about it."

They drove on in silence, Walker feeling strangely high. He was honored that Alec had chosen him to open up to, even if they hadn't really "talked." He guessed it was because Alec considered him non-judgemental. Friends had said that about him.

Around noon, the road descended into the Kwando River valley. The landscape abruptly changed from burnt orange to lush green. Cecil pulled under a jackalberry tree with a view of the winding river.

"We'll lunch here," he said.

As they ate in the shade of the jackalberry, the boys watched a fish eagle wheel over the river, uttering a thin, plaintive cry.

"So, where is the Angolan border?" Alec said.

"About thirty kilometers further on," Cecil said.

"And where did they see this antelope?"

"That was on the Kavango River. Another two hundred and forty kilometers."

"Two hundred forty?" Chas said. "That's like a hundred and fifty miles? Fuck!"

Cecil frowned. "Do you boys ever stop complaining? Christ!"

Back on the road, they left the green river valley and returned to the red, dry veldt. More bush, more nothing. Walker leaned his head against the window and began to doze.

"Whoa, what is this?" Alec said.

Walker snapped awake. It took him a moment to make

sense of what he was seeing—another Land Rover, upside down on the side of the road, like a beetle on its back. The smell of gasoline hung in the air.

Patrick frowned. "This is a SADF vehicle. Do you see the markings?"

Sure enough, the lettering was there on the side of the door. But what had happened to it? There was no crater in the road, no bullet holes that they could see.

"Might be some damage on the other side," Alec said.

For the first time he'd been in Africa, Walker felt truly afraid. Animals were more or less predictable. People were not.

"Patrick, do you think SWAPO did this?" Walker asked.

"SWAPO, yes. Quite likely."

Cecil stopped and waved for Patrick to come abreast. "That was an unpleasant surprise," he said.

"I don't think it's safe to drive this road," Patrick said. "We should turn around."

"We're not going back to Vic Falls," Cecil said. "We've come too far for that."

He pulled out his map and studied it. "Here's a secondary road that forks off and runs parallel to this one. Let's take that."

"But, sir, they said to stick to the main road."

"Yes, yes, I know, but there'll be more game on a side road. I'll keep an eye out for it."

A few miles along, they came to the side road. It was little more than a dirt track filled with potholes, but Cecil entered without hesitation. Patrick put his car into four wheel drive and followed.

As the Rover rocked from side to side, Walker surveyed the surroundings. Giant termite mounds stood like gnomes above the baked earth. The few standing trees were broken in half as if hit by shellfire. He asked Patrick if this was a sign of more fighting.

"No, this is elephant," Patrick said, "They break off the branches to get at the leaves."

"Wow, they're as bad as humans."

"They can be quite destructive, especially when they are too numerous."

Walker peered ahead, certain they would be seeing game. "Is it okay if I ride on top? We're going pretty slow."

"I should think so."

Patrick stopped the car. Walker grabbed his camera, slung it around his neck, and climbed onto the platform. He knocked twice on the roof and held on as the car moved forward.

From his elevated perch, he could see signs of elephants all around—piles of dung and broken trees. His pulse quickened. Up ahead, Cecil's brake lights came on. He must have seen something. Sure enough, there was an elephant just beside the road. Cecil slowly passed it and pulled over to the shoulder. Patrick came to a halt just short.

"Do you want a picture?" he called out the window.

"Yes, but don't get any closer," Walker said.

He focused the telephoto lens. The elephant was about a hundred feet away, a young male with two-foot-long tusks. At the sight of the Land Rovers, he raised his trunk and smelled the air. Great shot! The elephant swung his head toward the blue Rover, his trunk aimed straight at Walker. Did it smell him? The animal began swinging his head from side to side, scooping dirt off the ground and throwing it in the air.

Walker called down from the roof. "Better back up."

Patrick put the car into reverse and slowly retreated. The movement drew the elephant's ire. He strode out into the road. Then, he charged. Walker grabbed the roof rack as Patrick punched the accelerator. The engine whined, maxed out in reverse, yet the elephant was gaining on them. The car started swaying. Walker tightened his grip. The car jerked to a halt, and in an instant, he was catapulted backwards, landing hard in the middle of the dirt road.

Walker sat up and found himself looking at the back of the idling car. Where was the elephant? He heard a crunching of glass, saw the enraged beast ramming his tusks into the Rover's windshield. The elephant backed up, spotted Walker on the ground, and started toward him. Walker scrambled to his feet and ran to the opposite side of the car. The elephant kept coming. Walker circled to the front. The passenger side door flew open. Alec jumped out, grabbed him by the shirt collar, and hauled him over his lap into the front seat.

"Go! Go! Go!" Alec yelled.

Patrick put the car into first and sped forward. He shifted gears, glancing in the rear view mirror.

"Is he still behind us?" Alec said.

"He's slowing down," Patrick said.

"Are you sure?"

"Yes, he's going back to the bush."

Alec relaxed his grip on Walker's shirt. "You can get off me now," he said.

Walker pulled himself into the back seat next to Elliot. Feeling pain in his hands, he turned them over to find his palms scraped raw.

"Oh, shit!" Elliot said. "Are you going to need stitches?"

"No. Hurts, though."

With the elephant gone out of sight, Patrick slowed and came to a halt beside the red Rover. Cecil leaned out the window.

"Good, Christ, is everyone alright?" he said.

"Walker has injured his hands," Patrick said.

"Pull up ahead. I'll get out the First Aid kit."

Patrick drove to the shoulder and shut off the engine. "I'm sorry I stopped so suddenly," he said to Walker. "I lost control."

"It's okay," Walker said.

Elliot pointed at his camera. "Your telephoto is busted."

Walker fingered the cracked lens. "Shit. Now, I'm going to have to use the 50 millimeter."

"Fuck that," Alec said. "We've got a busted windshield."

It surely was broken, two baseball-sized holes with cracks spreading in all directions. This was bad. This was really bad.

Cecil arrived with the First Aid kit, Chas and Schwartzy right behind. Walker opened the door and held out his hands.

"Oh, gross!" Chas said.

Cecil took out a packet of gauze and began to wrap his wounds.

"God, I've never seen anything like that in my life," he said. "That elephant was completely mad!"

"He nearly got me," Walker said. "Alec saved my ass."

Alec offered a casual salute.

"Hey, Cecil," Chas said. "Was that the closest call you've ever had on any of your trips?"

"Yes, I'd say so."

"Too bad you didn't get it on film."

The boys laughed. Cecil ignored them and finished bandaging Walker's hands.

"There, now," he said. "That should do nicely."

"Shouldn't he go to a hospital?" Elliot said.

Cecil snapped the First Aid kit shut. "He's not that bad off. Now, let's have a look at this windshield."

Cecil walked around to the front of the car and ran a hand over the cracks. He gave the windshield a gentle push.

"It seems to be holding," he said. "Can you see well enough to drive, Patrick?"

"Yes, but it will soon get worse," Patrick said.

"We have to keep going," Cecil said. "We don't have any other choice."

With that, Cecil returned to his car. Walker and Patrick exchanged glances in the mirror. The wounded and the silenced, their fate was in the hands of this crazy man. In fact, they had no choice but to follow.

※

Late in the afternoon, Cecil came to a halt. He leaned out the window and studied the terrain. It looked to Walker as before—termite mounds and broken trees. But among them stood a pair of healthy acacias and, underneath, a patch of bare ground that would do for a campsite. Cecil and Patrick drove the cars through the grass and parked them at right angles, forming one half of a defensive perimeter. The boys took over from there, dragging branches from the surrounding forest to build a wall enclosing the campsite.

With his damaged palms, Walker could only supervise.

"Cut some thorn branches and work them in between," he said to Schwartzy.

Cecil watched with apparent amusement. "You realize you can't stop everything," he said to the boys. "This is Africa after all."

"We can try," Walker said.

While Cecil fixed dinner, Schwartzy scaled one of the acacias and scanned the surrounding bush.

"See anything?" Walker asked.

"A couple of warthogs," Schwartzy said.

Chas sniffed. "Warthogs. I hate warthogs."

That night, as he lay in his cot, Walker opened his *Thoreau* and read an essay entitled "Ktaadn." The author spoke about getting lost in a tangle of brush on the legendary mountain's flanks.

Perhaps I most fully realized that this was primeval, untamed, and forever untamable Nature...We have not seen Nature unless we have seen her thus vast and drear and inhuman. This was Earth of which we have heard, made out of Chaos and Old Night. Here was no man's garden, but the unhandselled globe.

He closed the book. Thoreau was losing his faith. The essay spelled it out as clear as day. How was it that so many people were unaware of this? Why had they made the man out to be a prophet?

From out of the dark came an ominous sound—*Huh! Huh! Huh!* A grunt more than a roar, it seemed unfathomably deep and uncomfortably close.

"Is that a lion?" he said.

Cecil answered in a giddy voice. "Yes! Quite a big one, I'd say."

Walker aimed his flashlight toward the makeshift barrier. They'd left an opening about two feet wide to allow people to come and go.

"Should we close that gap?" he said.

"A lion's not going to wander into an enclosure," Cecil said. "It's not in their nature."

"Are you sure about that?"

"Quite. Now, go back to sleep."

Sleep didn't come easily. Walker kept imagining the creature just on the other side of the perimeter, smelling their sweaty bodies, looking for a way in. But Cecil knew lions better than he did. Hopefully, he was right about their sensibilities.

Somewhere in the night, he woke up, dreaming that the lion was inside the compound. He flicked on his flashlight and shone it around. Elliot's cot was empty. He got up and shone the light into the cars. Not there. He went to the opening and took a few steps outside. There was Elliot, standing in his underwear, face to face with an enormous maned lion.

Without thinking, Walker ran forward, shouting in his deepest voice. "Get outta here! Get! Get!"

The lion turned and ran. He grabbed Elliot and pulled him back towards the compound.

"Are you out of your mind?" he said.

Flashlights popped on as he came inside.

"What's happened?" Cecil said.

"Elliot was sleepwalking again. He was standing right in front of a fucking lion!"

"Good, Christ!"

"Baas, I think we need to close this fence," Patrick said.

"Yes, that's fine."

Now, the others were up, helping Patrick arrange the branches to close the gap.

"I want you sleeping in the Land Rover from now on,"

Cecil said to Elliot. "I can't have you wandering off in the middle of the night."

Elliot picked up his sleeping bag and headed for the red Rover.

"I'm going in, too," Chas said. "Enough of this shit."

Others began grabbing their sleeping bags.

"I'm going inside."

"Me, too."

"Everyone can't fit in the cars," Cecil said. "Some of you will have to sleep on the roofs."

Schwartzy turned to Walker. "I'll go on top. Do you want to come?"

"Yes! Which car?"

"Let's take the red."

Alec turned to Patrick. "Do you want to join me in the blue car?"

"If you don't mind."

"Grab your bag. Let's go."

Soon, only Cecil remained on the ground. The car doors shut. The silence returned. Walker tossed back and forth, staring up at the tree branches silhouetted against the sky. He heard what he thought might be another animal, maybe a warthog. But it was Cecil snoring, dreaming no doubt about his beloved Africa.

Chapter 20

Josiah, Johannes, and Petras arrived back at their base, dragging Emmanuel's body. They had pulled him by his feet, forcing his shirt over his head and revealing the gaping wounds in his chest. Other soldiers stared as they entered the compound, turning away at the realization that their comrade was dead.

Josiah stopped in front of command headquarters. He pulled Emmanuel's shirt down over his chest and wiped the grass and dirt off his face. The dead were nothing but pieces of meat. He went inside to face his captain.

The man listened impassively as Josiah explained the details of the mission.

"You did not plant the road mine?" the captain said.

"No, sir, we did not."

"So, you failed in your mission."

"Yes, sir."

"Were you followed? The enemy was no doubt alerted to your presence because you fired your weapons."

"No, sir. After we crossed the river, we hid in the bush and waited for some time but did not see any activity."

The captain nodded. "Let's see your man."

Flies swarmed around Emmanuel's face. Josiah hurried to wave them off. The commander studied the wounds in his chest.

"An elephant did this?"

"Yes, sir."

"Fucking beasts. We should kill them all."

The captain instructed Johannes and Petras to bury Emmanuel. "Corporal," he said to Josiah, "You may stand down until tomorrow."

Josiah returned to his barracks and collapsed on his bunk and wept. He was exhausted, wracked with guilt. He pictured Emmanuel's mother wailing. She would wonder about her son's last moments. He needed to write her a letter and explain what happened. He would do that tomorrow.

He fell into a fitful sleep, periodically aware of other soldiers entering the barracks. Then, nothing, until a strange sound entered his dreams. A tokoloshe, a humanoid creature in Zulu mythology, was screaming, warning of more death. Who was this woman? Where did she come from?

The explosion knocked him from his bunk and set his ears ringing. He came awake and saw men running towards the door, their clothes on fire. Smoke began to fill the room. He struggled to his feet and staggered outside in his underwear. Men poured out of the barracks into the parade ground, some with shattered arms and legs, burned faces and hands. He could not understand what had happened, and then he heard the high-pitched whine return. Through the trees, he glimpsed a jet airplane turning towards him. SADF!

As the jet approached, some men began to run for

the bush. Others aimed rifles skyward. Unarmed, worthless to the fight, Josiah was determined not to flee. The sleek monster grew, and opened its belly. Out came half a dozen bombs, hurtling downwards. The explosions shattered the guard tower and proceeded in a line across the parade ground, obliterating some men and launching others like rag dolls. Screams filled the air. Bodies writhed on the ground. He remained frozen.

Then something else happened. The bush at the edge of the base filled with a crackling like fireworks, and men who had been uninjured by the bombs began to fall. They were under attack from the ground! As more men fell, the enemy began emerging from the bush. White and black faces, firing automatic weapons. Black soldiers killing their Black brothers!

Josiah decided to run. Past the burning barracks and through the tattered barbed wire. He fled into the bush, flinging branches aside, thorns and all. Obstacles were his friend—anything to put distance and barriers between him and the attackers.

The firing seemed to be fading. He stopped to catch his breath, hands on knees. He turned and looked behind him. No one was coming. Somehow, he had escaped. He considered what had just happened. The South African Defense Force had crossed the border and bombed Angolan soil. This never happened while the Portuguese military were present, but with their departure, all bets were off. PLAN no longer had a sanctuary.

He crouched on the ground for a long time, not moving. Doves landed in the tree above him and commenced their soft cooing. A tiny antelope, a dik-dik, emerged from the bush and began feeding not ten yards away. He marveled at the animal's huge dark eyes and short, slender legs. This creature, like him, must live in constant fear. Every manner of cat, jackal, hyena, and eagle preyed on duiker. Humans did, too, with their cruel snares.

Ants crawling up his naked legs forced him to scratch. The duiker ran. The doves flew. It was time for him to move, as well. He could only think of returning to the base. Where else could he go? He darted from bush to bush, stopping to check for any movement. He saw smoke rising above the trees. And, finally, the base—a collection of smoldering ruins surrounded by bodies. Dozens of bodies.

A handful of armed soldiers moved slowly among the dead. He watched until he was sure they were PLAN. And then he emerged. The soldiers seemed oblivious to his presence. They were in shock, staring at their fallen comrades. Some of the bodies were burned beyond description. Others were recognizable. Here was Petras with half a dozen bullets through his chest. And Johannes with a mangled foot and a hole in his forehead. He looked to have been executed at close range. The South Africans were monsters. They must be made to pay!

"Corporal Hangula!"

The captain approached, his face contorted with rage. Josiah came to attention and saluted.

"Jou gek! You fool! You were followed!"

"Sir?"

"Do you think it was a coincidence that we were attacked the day after your bungled mission? I should have you shot!"

The words sank in. It was true. He had not, in fact, waited across the river. As soon as he and his men reached the far shore, they dragged Emmanuel through the bush, leaving a trail of blood even a child could follow. His head began to spin. He had killed almost his entire platoon.

"Sir, I am guilty. You may shoot me now."

"Shut up! I need every uninjured man I can find, even the useless ones." Sucking his teeth in disgust, the captain stared at the bodies. "Find a man with a bullet hole through his chest. There should be plenty of them. Strip off his uniform and wear it. For the rest of your miserable life, I want you to be reminded of what you've done."

Chapter 21

Patrick felt sick to his stomach. He had nearly killed Walker by slamming on the brakes and sending him flying onto the road. He hadn't known any other way to stop the Rover from tipping over, but if he'd been a better driver, it wouldn't have swayed in the first place. And now the windshield was shattered. The memory of the enraged elephant's eyes, the tusk that burst through the glass just centimeters from his face...*He* could easily have been killed.

Cecil's mission to find this antelope was foolish. Yes, the giant sable was special, but why drive a thousand kilometers through a war zone just to find this one? "There are lots of sable antelope back in Rhodesia," Patrick said to Cecil. "Some quite big."

"Yes, but not like this Angolan subspecies," Cecil countered. "It's a head taller than the common sable and has absolutely enormous horns—a hundred and sixty-five centimeters for a big male. That's over five feet long!"

Patrick nodded. "I've never seen a sable antelope of that size."

Cecil went on. "I stand to be the first person to ever film one in the wild, and quite possibly the last. With

Angola headed for chaos, the remaining population could be wiped out in a year's time!"

"But we are not going into Angola," Patrick said. "It is too dangerous."

Cecil nodded. "Of course not. But this one animal was spotted right on the border, on the north bank of the Kavango River. What it was doing there, I can't imagine. That's eight hundred kilometers south of its normal range. But I simply must try to get a photograph of it. I'd become quite famous. So would you, I might add."

Patrick, famous? It was possible. If they actually managed to find this animal, he would be known as the guide who helped lead the expedition. That could be good for business. Very good.

That night, they all sat around the campfire recounting the day's excitement.

"Man, you went flying off that roof!" Chas said to Walker. "You could have easily broken your neck."

"Then the elephant came after you," Elliot said. "I thought he was going to get you."

Walker nodded. "I tried to keep the car between him and me, but that elephant was quick. Alec saved my ass by pulling me inside."

"And you, man," Alec said to Patrick. "You did a great job backing that Land Rover. I don't care what you say."

Patrick blushed. "Thank you, Alec."

As Patrick stared into the fire, a strange shape began to emerge from somewhere behind it—a giant orb the color of the flames.

"What is this?" he said to the others. "Do you see?"

Cecil, sitting to one side, called out. "Why, it's the moon! Come over here. You can see it. A bloody full moon!"

Patrick gasped. This had to be a sign. The San people, those !Gubi that they had seen in the desert, considered the moon a trickster. What this spirit was up to, he could only guess.

Patrick awoke the next morning to a strange sound, a bookend to the blood-red moon. Two jet airplanes passed low overhead in close formation, their high-pitched engines shattering the silence of the veldt. He was familiar with the commercial jets that came in and out of Windhoek airport, but these were something different—straight-winged, windowless craft painted a somber gray.

The boys saw them, too, and were on their feet in an instant.

"Cool!" Elliot said. "Bombers!"

"Those are Canberras," Cecil said. "They're made in Britain."

Patrick had no doubt about whom these bombers belonged to. South Africa was the only country in the vicinity that had those kinds of airplanes. But where were they going, and where had they been?

After breakfast, they packed up the cars and headed back on the road, Walker and Chas as Patrick's passengers. Today, they would reach the Kavango River and the town of Divundu. Patrick hoped they would stop there to get the windshield repaired. He could see the cracks spreading.

Walker, seated next to him, put his hand to the glass. "Do you think it's going to hold?"

"I don't know. It's getting worse."

"If it goes, will the whole thing go at once?"

"It's possible."

An hour down the road, they came to the bridge over the Kavango. Cecil drove to the middle of the span, stopped, and got out of his car.

"Isn't this exciting!" he said. "The Kavango River!"

Patrick joined him at the railing. The river was impressive—some hundred yards wide, dark, almost black, winding toward the town of Divundu.

"Will we stop here to repair the windshield?" he asked.

Cecil frowned. "I'd like to get to Mbane. It's likely to take at least a day to repair it, and I don't want to be stuck here."

"What if it collapses on the way there?" Walker said. "The cracks are spreading."

Cecil walked over and studied the windshield. He pushed on the glass.

"It seems to be holding just fine. Can you see alright to drive, Patrick?"

"It is difficult, but yes, I can see."

"Let's move on, then."

The road they followed paralleled the river, which came in and out of view between a border of trees. They would be across from Angola now. Patrick thought of Josiah, hopefully safe on that far shore. When they reached Mbane, he would try to get a message to their mother to find out if she'd heard anything about him.

The land they passed through bore little evidence of actual conflict. The pastures along the river were green, but the entrance gates to the White-owned farms were closed, with "Trespassers Will Be Shot" signs nailed to the posts.

The local Africans were still here. A collection of

circular mud huts with thatched roofs appeared beside the road. Women with bodies tinted a flat shade of ochre stood watching. Some were bare-breasted, their hair pleated in braids covered with red mud.

"Check this out!" Chas said. "I'm seeing some titties!"

"These are Himba people," Patrick said. "They are pastoralists. They cover their skin with a paste to protect themselves from the sun and flies."

"What's up with the hair?" Walker said.

"The braids are meant to hide the face and breasts. They are worn by unmarried girls as a sign of modesty."

Chas sniffed. "Screw the braids. Let's see some more skin."

The village fell behind. The empty land resumed.

Finally, they came to a sign announcing their arrival in Mbane.

Walker sounded out the name. "Meh-ban. Is that how it's pronounced?"

"Mm-beh-neh," Patrick corrected him.

Pedestrians lined the road—men carrying wooden staffs, women with plastic jugs on their heads. Small shops appeared, their open fronts revealing items for sale—bags of charcoal, sundries, bicycle tires. Up ahead, Cecil slowed and leaned out the window. He asked a man for directions. The man pointed down the street. They proceeded a few blocks and arrived at a white cinderblock building—the police station.

"Come with me," Cecil said to Patrick. "I'll need you to help explain what happened."

Patrick felt nervous about this. Would he be blamed for the accident? A blemish placed on his record? The waiting room inside was hot and close. A uniformed Black man sat behind a protective window. Cecil bent down to speak through the circular opening.

"I'd like to file an accident report," he said.

The man directed them to an office where Officer De Kok, a large, uniformed White man sat behind a desk, a portable fan blowing across his sweating face. He urged them to take a seat.

"How can I help you?" he said to Cecil.

"We had a bit of an accident," Cecil said. "No other vehicles involved, but I'd like to file a report so I can get an insurance claim."

"What kind of accident was it?"

"We were attacked by an elephant. Damnedest thing I've ever seen. Charged one of my cars for no good reason. Patrick here backed away as fast as he could, but it just kept coming. Smashed his tusks right through the windshield!"

The officer raised his eyebrows. "What kind was it? Male, female?"

"A young male. I'd say about fifteen years old, wouldn't you, Patrick?"

"Yes, baas. A young male."

"We've had big trouble with rogue elephants of late," the officer said. "Most likely, his parents were shot. Without adult supervision, young males misbehave. Just like our teenagers."

Cecil nodded. "Quite. Who's been doing the shooting?"

"Natives shoot them for trampling their gardens. Poachers shoot them for their ivory. Rumor has it SADF is shooting them for target practice. We've got no game wardens up here. The situation is bloody out of control."

"Oh, blast."

The officer opened a drawer and took out a form. "Where did this happen?"

"About a hundred kilometers east. Not far from Divundu."

"Let's have a look at your driver's licenses."

They fished out their wallets. "Patrick was the driver of the damaged car. I'm the owner."

De Kok studied Cecil's license. "England? Are you some kind of tourist?"

"I'm a filmmaker, actually. I've got a bunch of boys with me. They've come all the way from America!"

"Which way did you come in from?"

"Vic Falls."

The officer frowned. "That road is supposed to be closed to anyone but locals. Did they not tell you that?"

"Yes, but I've got special permission. I came here to try and film that giant sable antelope. I'm sure you've heard about it."

"Heard about it, yes. That was on the Angolan side of the river, and you're not going over there. SADF has a strict policy—no crossing the river. Anyone who tries will be arrested. Anyone who resists will be shot."

"Oh, dear."

"My advice to you is to head back to Windhoek as soon as you get that windshield fixed. We've got big trouble brewing. Since the Portuguese pulled out of Angola, the rebels have been setting up bases there. They've been coming across the river at night, planting mines and whatnot. We've lost several officers."

"Yes, well...Might I ask exactly where the antelope was seen?"

The officer narrowed his eyes. "That was upriver. Where the Cuanavale meets the Kavango."

The officer stood and tapped the form on the desk. "Let's have a look at that car."

※

By a stroke of luck, the Portuguese auto shop in Mbane had a windshield for the Land Rover. With the military in town, they'd stocked up on parts. But they would not be able to install it until the following day.

Cecil frowned. "I guessed as much. Are there any campsites in the area? I'd like to be by the river."

The shop owner answered in a thick Portuguese accent. "There is a few fish camps, but everything is now close-ed up. You can maybe find someone to let you stay in their yard."

Patrick followed Cecil as they drove to the end of town facing the river. A rutted side road led to a neighborhood of tin-roofed huts along the bluff. He put the Rover in four-wheel drive and inched forward. Black faces stared at the improbable visitors. In an empty lot, children chased a soccer ball made of plastic bags bound up in twine.

They came to the end of the road, to an open area overlooking the river. Cecil stepped out and surveyed the scene. It was strewn with garbage but could conceivably fit their group.

"Could you ask one of these people if we could camp here?" Cecil said to Patrick. "I rather doubt they speak English."

Patrick spotted a woman peering out the doorway of the nearest hut. He addressed her in Silozi. "Shangwe Ima! Can we camp over there?"

Yes, they could camp there.

"Fabulous," Cecil said. "Boys, unload the cars."

Chas stepped out. "Oh, this is special. A scenic landfill."

The group kicked aside tin cans and beer bottles and spread out their cots. Cecil strolled to the edge of the bluff and gazed down at the river. On the shore beneath the huts were several canoes. A Black man sat by one mending his fishing net.

"Patrick, come here. I'd like to ask this man something."

They sidled down the bluff and walked over to the man.

Cecil introduced himself. "Hello. I'm Cecil Covington. I'm from England."

"Wayakura," the man said. Welcome.

"I've come all the way here to photograph the giant sable antelope." He held his hands atop his head, imitating a pair of horns. "Do you know of this animal? I've heard one has been seen across the river."

Patrick translated. "Yes, he knows of this creature. He has seen it."

"He's *seen* it? Where exactly?"

The man pointed upriver.

"He saw it two days ago," Patrick said. "Walking along the far shore."

"Are you sure it was a giant sable and not some other antelope?"

The man nodded vigorously. "Niti? Sumbakaloko!"

Cecil's eyes sparkled. "Ask him if he will take me across the river in his canoe. Tell him I will pay him thirty rands."

The man shook his head.

"No, he will not take you. It is strictly forbidden to cross the river."

"Tell him fifty."

The man was unmoved.

"He will not do it," Patrick said. "He says he could have his canoe confiscated by the military, might be put in jail."

"Bloody hell. Alright, let's go and drop the car off."

Leaving the boys at camp, he and Cecil drove both vehicles to the auto shop. Patrick parked the damaged Rover and climbed into the front seat of Cecil's. On the ride back, Cecil was silent. The man looked terribly sad, his shoulders hunched, his thin lips in a frown. He'd come all this way with such high hopes. And to know that fame resided just across the river.

Patrick reached out and patted him on the shoulder. "I am sad, too, baas."

Cecil teared up. "Yes, yes. Thank you. We've tried our best, haven't we?"

They turned into the muddy lane and drove past the line of huts. Cecil brightened. "Perhaps I should ask one of the other boat owners if he would take me."

"No one will take you, baas. The boats are too expensive, and they do not want to risk their lives."

"What if I offered to buy one?"

"A canoe?"

"Yes. And paddle it over myself."

"You could not paddle one of those canoes alone. They are too heavy."

"What if you were to come with me? Would you be willing to do that?"

Patrick felt the blood rising in his head. "Baas, this puts me in a difficult position."

"Yes, of course. I shouldn't have asked."

What a manipulator this man was. But what choice did he, Patrick, really have? If he were to say no, Cecil would be crushed. The man would live the rest of his life thinking that he'd had a real shot at fame. And he, Patrick, as well. This was *his* shot.

"If you can buy a canoe, I will go with you," Patrick said.

Cecil smiled. "Oh, jolly good. I knew you'd come around."

Patrick shook his head. What had he just agreed to?

They arrived back at camp to find Walker, Paul, and Alec playing soccer with the children. He was surprised to see Alec doing this, even more surprised to see a smile on the boy's face.

Cecil parked the car. "Let's see if we can find the owner of that canoe. What do you think I should offer him?"

Patrick pondered. "I would say five hundred rands."

"Good Lord. I don't know if I have that much cash."

They walked down the bank and along the line of mud and thatch huts. It was nearing dinner time, and smoke from the charcoal cookstoves was rising out of the courtyards and drifting across the river. They found the man sitting on his grass mat. Cecil took out his wallet and presented a fat wad of bills.

"I will offer you five hundred rands for your canoe," he said. "If I should lose it, you can use this money to buy a new one. If I bring it back, you are welcome to have the dugout canoe *and* the money."

The man leafed through the bills. He looked Cecil in the eye, smiled, and clapped his hands in thanks. "Shangwe!!!"

"Yes," Patrick said. "He will sell it!"

Chapter 22

Walker was flabbergasted when he heard that Cecil had bought a canoe and intended to paddle it across the river with Patrick. It wasn't just that they might be arrested, but that they might tip over and drown. The canoe appeared to have been carved out of a tree. It was at least eighteen feet long with low sides and boards for seats. The two paddles were crude affairs—long and thin with spoon-shaped blades.

"Have either of you ever paddled a canoe before?" Walker said.

Patrick shook his head, no. Cecil offered that he'd gone punting on the River Cam in Cambridge. Walker explained that it was not the same thing. Canoes could be very tippy for the inexperienced and big rivers like the Kavango had a deceptively strong current. Walker knew. He'd paddled a canoe in summer camp across many kinds of rivers and lakes.

"You should at least try it out first," he said.

In the fading light, the three of them carried the canoe down to the shore and set it in the water. Cecil climbed in the back seat, Patrick in front. They started to paddle and immediately began tipping from side to side. Walker waded out to steady the boat.

"Don't paddle," he said. "Take a minute to find your balance."

Cecil and Patrick sat with their paddles across the gunwales.

"Okay, try it now."

The men headed out into the river. Cecil kept switching sides to try and keep the canoe running straight, but it veered in the current and drifted downstream. There was no way they could make it all the way across the river.

"Come on back!" Walker said.

Cecil stepped out of the boat looking uneasy. "We'll try it again in the morning," he said.

That evening, the boys made a fire atop the bluff. They sat in a circle, saying little. Walker picked up his book, then tossed it aside. Thoreau would not be his savior. Nature was not the answer. In the past week, he'd seen forests destroyed by elephants and witnessed a crocodile devour a mother cheetah, leaving her kittens to die a miserable death. In some ways, he felt he was back to where he was upon his arrival to the continent—questioning the existence of God, the purpose of life. And yet this trip had given him an eagerness to live. His brief but heartfelt exchange with Alec convinced him that he had something to offer, sympathies and skills that he could share with others to better their lives in some small fashion.

He glanced at Cecil, downcast face reflected in the firelight. Walker had forgiven the man his errant kiss. Cecil had his faults, but he was not a predator. He'd shown the boys a magnificent time and instilled in them a love for travel, for adventure. Not just this group, but a dozen groups before. Would Cecil consider it all a waste if he could not at least catch a glimpse of the giant sable?

"Cecil," Walker said. "How about I paddle you across the river?"

Cecil looked up. "Really? What about your hands?"

"They're not too bad. I can manage."

"Oh, that would be marvelous!"

Now, Patrick was enlivened. "I will come, too," he said. "You may need someone who speaks Silozi. I will paddle in front."

Walker nodded. "That's a good idea. Cecil can sit in the middle with his camera. If we see the sable from the river, he could film it."

Schwartzy looked concerned. "Are you sure about this, Walker? It's not like you to take a big risk. Your dad would be totally opposed."

"Yes, I'm sure."

But that night, he couldn't sleep. He played out different scenarios for the following day. They could be stopped by SADF and thrown in jail. They could tip over in midriver and be eaten by crocodiles. What a horrible way to die!

Cecil woke him in the predawn darkness. "Time to get up," he said. "We should eat something and get across the river before sunup."

Walker put on his clothes. He had no appetite, but Cecil convinced him to eat a banana. At least that would calm his innards.

While the others slept, he, Cecil, and Patrick made their way down to the river. Walker held the canoe while Cecil settled into the middle and Patrick in the bow. He pushed the boat into knee-deep water, then climbed aboard.

"Alright, let's go," he said.

He started with delicate strokes, not wanting to risk an upset. The river was black, indistinguishable from shore and sky. He felt suspended in space, unmoored from the known world. Water dripped from the paddle as he swung it forward, a sound like beads sliding down a string.

"You're doing marvelously!" Cecil whispered.

A loud splash ripped the silence. Walker jerked upright, stared in the direction of the sound.

"What was that?" he said.

"I think it is a fish," Patrick said.

Long minutes passed before he could settle down. The shore should be coming into view, but where was it?

And then they were there, skidding to a halt in the mud. A white fog hid the contours of the land.

"Do you want to get out, Cecil?" he said.

"No, let's paddle along the shore. The junction with the Cuanavale is upstream. That's where the sable was last seen."

Walker backed the canoe off the mud and turned upstream, leaning into his stroke to counteract the slow but steady current. The light was coming up now. He could make out a sandbar up ahead.

"Let's get out here," Cecil said. "We'll look for tracks."

They stepped onto the sandbar and fanned out in different directions. Tracks were abundant, mostly small—warthog, dik-dik, monkey.

"Look here!" Cecil said. "This is an antelope. A big one."

Walker examined the track—a heart-shaped depression nearly as big as his hand. It looked fresh, no more than a day old. He peered across the bar to the wooded bank. Was that a horn? No, just a branch stripped of bark.

"Let's keep going," Cecil said. "We're not quite at the junction."

They got back in the canoe and paddled upstream. As quiet as they were, they might actually be able to get close to this antelope. But where was it?

Patrick sat up and pointed. "Look! Just there!"

It took Walker a moment to discern the jet black animal from the dark wall of the forest. The white stripes on its face and white belly gave it away. It was walking slowly along the head-high bank, oblivious to their presence.

"That's it!" Cecil breathed. "That's a giant sable!"

He peered through the viewfinder of his camera. "We need to get closer."

Using his gentlest stroke, Walker moved the canoe toward the shore. Cecil began filming, the rattle of the Bolex' motor breaking the silence. It was really happening!

They were within a hundred feet now. Walker could see every feature—the long legs, the dark eyes, the massive, backward curving horns. It was a bull, for sure. The sable stopped and stared. Not at them, but something up ahead. Just like that, he disappeared into the forest.

"Quick, let's get to shore!" Cecil said.

They landed on the beach and jumped out of the canoe. Cecil led the way, his camera held at the ready. They were running now, closing in on the spot, when four soldiers with AK47s emerged from the trees. Walker skidded to a halt. The soldiers stopped.

One man, the squad leader, held his hand in the air. "Shoot them!" he said.

Somehow, Walker knew it would end like this. Their headlong pursuit of this will-o'-the-wisp, their sense of invincibility, their ignorance of the depths of Africa's human conflicts—all this had led them up a blind alley. And now they were powerless.

"Shoot!" the man repeated.

One soldier—a man with a strangely familiar face—pointed at Patrick. "Captain, this man is my brother."

The captain scowled. "Are you going to mess things up again, Corporal?"

"No, sir. This is my brother. He is a safari guide from Windhoek."

The captain called Patrick forward. "You are a guide? Show me your ID."

Patrick produced his wallet.

"Patrick Hangula. What are you doing in Angola?"

"We are looking for the giant sable antelope. It was just here."

"An *antelope*? You can find antelope in Etosha. Thousands of them."

The captain drew a pistol and planted it on Patrick's forehead. "I think you are Boer spies."

"No, sir. Please!"

Walker waited for the shot to ring out. Then, Cecil started talking, his voice filled with righteous anger.

"This is not just any antelope," he said. "This is the giant sable! It's revered by you people. And I've just gotten the first footage ever." He held his camera up. "I would have taken more, but you scared him away!"

Walker couldn't believe it. Cecil was admonishing their would-be killer, whose face now swelled with rage. *Give him something*, Walker thought. *Give him something.*

"Sir, it's true," he said to the captain. "Cecil has photographed this animal. He'll give you the film. You can take it and show it to your leaders. They'll thank you for it."

The captain's expression softened. "Give me the camera," he said.

Cecil clutched it to his chest.

"Give it to me, or I'll shoot!"

Hand opening like that of a dying man, Cecil let go of the Bolex. The captain turned it over and fiddled with the latch.

"Don't open it here," Cecil said. "You'll ruin the film!"

Patrick stepped forward and touched Cecil's shoulder. "Baas, we must leave now."

Cecil hesitated.

"Baas! Now!"

Patrick backed away, drawing Cecil with him. Walker followed suit. The soldiers watched them go.

⚯

The boys stood atop the bluff, waving frantically. As soon as the dugout canoe touched the shore, they ran down.

Schwartzy grabbed the bow. "What took you so long?" he said. "We were getting worried!"

Patrick stepped out, knelt down on the ground, and began to pray.

"Whoa," Schwartzy said. "What happened?"

Cecil raised his hand. "Somebody help me up."

Elliot obliged, pulling Cecil to his feet. "Did you see it? Did you see the giant sable?" he said.

Cecil didn't answer.

"Yes, we saw it," Walker said. "Cecil actually filmed it. Then, we ran into trouble."

He went on to relate how they were confronted by the PLAN rebels and how they were about to be shot when one of the soldiers recognized Patrick as his brother.

"For real, dude?" Chas said to Patrick. "You ran into your brother?"

"Yes."

"He's a PLAN combatant?"

Patrick nodded.

Chas stared across the river as if just now taking in the larger world. "And they just let you go?"

"They were hesitating," Walker said. "The leader thought we might be spies. Cecil told them about the giant sable, how important it was, and that he had the first-ever footage. He gave them the camera to take back to Angola."

"You gave them the *camera*?" Schwartzy said to Cecil. "With the footage of the giant sable?"

Cecil frowned. "It wasn't my idea."

Schwartzy looked at Walker. "What's going on? Was this your idea?"

"We had to give them something," Walker said. "We were going to be shot!"

"You didn't know that," Cecil said. He pushed past the boys and started up the hill.

Walker's heart sank. What was he supposed to have done?

Schwartzy put a hand on his shoulder. "Come on," he said. "We've got something to show you."

Walker followed the others up the bluff and there, next to the red Rover, was the fully repaired blue car.

Cecil stared in disbelief. "How did this get here?"

"Alec hitchhiked to town and drove it back," Elliot said. "He thought you'd appreciate it."

"How did you pay for it?"

"I didn't," Alec said. "I told them you'd pay for it on

the way out of town."

Cecil walked up and examined the windshield. "Looks like they did a good job."

Alec nodded. "Yeah, I checked it out first."

"Why, thank you, Alec. That's ... that's quite nice."

Alec gave his casual salute. Cecil turned to Patrick.

"Let's return that canoe," he said. "We won't be needing it anymore."

"I'll help you," Walker said.

They climbed down the bank and pulled the canoe along the shore to just below the man's house. He was out front, as usual, mending nets.

"I've brought your canoe back," Cecil said. "Spic and span!"

The man stood and examined the canoe. He went to his shed and came back with the money, all five hundred rands. Cecil peeled off a hundred and handed it back.

"This is for rent," Cecil said.

The man smiled. "Luitumezi. Shangwe." Thank you.

Back at camp, Cecil announced it was time to pack up. "Let's make it quick," he said. "I want to make it to Grootfontein for the night."

Walker packed up his gear and stood for a moment looking at the two cars.

Schwartzy glanced over. "Who are you riding with?"

"I think I'll go with Patrick. Cecil's still pissed at me."

"Yeah, I wouldn't let that sit too long."

Walker considered Schwartzy's advice. Cecil was loading the red Land Rover by himself. Better go over and talk to him.

"Can I help you with anything?" Walker said.

Cecil avoided eye contact. "You can load the water jugs," he said.

Walker retrieved the empty jerry cans and set them on the roof rack.

"Listen, I'm sorry about the camera," he said. "It just came to me to offer it to them."

"I shan't blame you for it," Cecil said. "I suppose it's fair payback for what I did on the island."

"What? No, I don't hold that against you."

Cecil looked at him. "Really?"

"Not anymore. I mean, I did. For a while."

They continued loading the car.

"And, hey, you've still got the Livingstone initials," Walker said. "Those are important. They'll be a hit back in London."

Cecil managed a smile. "Yes. I've got you to thank for that."

"And don't give up on the film. Those guys might just get it developed. It could end up in a museum or something."

Cecil scoffed. "Just as easily, they'll be killed in battle and the film burnt to a crisp."

"Let's hope not."

Satisfied that he'd cleared the air, Walker returned to get his gear. He chose to ride in Patrick's Rover, along with Alec and Elliot. Best to let things with Cecil cool off.

Patrick started the car and followed Cecil to the auto shop. Cecil paid the bill, then led the way out of town.

The countryside south of Mbane was much the same as they'd seen for the past week—flat, dry bush, termite mounds, and scattered acacia trees. The road ran arrow straight across the endless plain, devoid of houses, devoid of traffic. Walker glanced in the rearview mirror and saw Patrick's eyes starting to flutter. He tapped Alec on the shoulder and nodded toward their driver.

"Hey, Patrick," Alec said. "I hear we're going to drop you off in Windhoek."

Patrick came fully awake. "Yes, Cecil has told me this. He said you are going to drive this car to Cape Town."

"Yeah, he finally trusts me."

Patrick smiled. He looked in the mirror. "I will miss you boys," he said.

"We'll miss you, too," Alec said.

Alec turned and nodded at Elliot, who pulled out his wallet. The boys had each contributed a hundred rands as a tip for Patrick.

"We've got something for you," Elliot said. "This is from all of us."

He handed Patrick the money.

"Oh, my goodness," Patrick said. "Thank you!"

Alec then reached into his own pocket and, to Walker's surprise, handed Patrick another five hundred rands.

"But this is too much!" Patrick said.

"No problem. I sold the pistol."

Walker leaned forward. "You sold the pistol?"

"To the mechanic at the auto shop."

"I thought Cecil hid it."

"Not well enough," Alec said.

Patrick laughed. "Not well enough," he said. "Not well enough."

"Now that you're rich, are you going to buy that Land Rover?" Alec said. "Start your own business?"

"Yes, I will do this," Patrick said. "I will wait until the troubles are over."

"What do you think's going to happen?" Walker said.

Patrick frowned. "I don't know. I think there will be

much fighting. Many people will die."

The car fell silent. Walker thought of the Appletons and their prosperous farm. He thought of Olivia. He thought of all the Africans they'd seen—the city dwellers in fashionable suits and dresses, the joyful musicians, the children in hand-me-down clothes kicking a soccer ball made of rags.

"Well, I hope you win," Alec said. "I hope you get your independence."

"And I hope your brother makes it back okay," Walker said. "If you see him, thank him for saving our lives."

"Yes, thank you. I will tell him."

They were silent for a time, the wheels crackling atop the gravel road.

"Hey, look!" Elliot said. "A rhinoceros! Can we stop and take a picture?"

Far out on the treeless plain, a hulking figure shambled head down toward an uncertain destination. Walker had been eager to see a rhinoceros, the only one of the Big Five he had yet to photograph. But the light was bad, the animal was far in the distance, and they had many, many miles to go.

"Fuck the rhino," he said. "Let's go home."

Epilogue

Following its declaration of independence in 1975, Angola descended into civil war. The primary combatants were the People's Movement for the Liberation of Angola (MPLA) and the National Union for the Total Independence of Angola (UNITA). MPLA wanted a communist form of government. Its soldiers were armed by the Soviet Union and assisted by Cuban soldiers on the ground. UNITA was backed by South Africa and the United States. The civil war lasted 27 years, destroyed Angola's infrastructure, and left nearly one million dead. Following the assassination of UNITA leader Joseph Savimbi in 2002, MPLA and UNITA signed a peace agreement, and the war ended. Angola is now a presidential constitutional republic.

In Namibia, fighting between SWAPO combatants and SADF forces increased sharply after 1975. In 1978, the United Nations Security Council passed Resolution 435, calling for elections under UN supervision and the cessation of all hostilities. However, South Africa refused to relinquish control of the country, and a decade of negotiations followed. A constitution was finally established in

1999, and Namibia was declared independent. Namibia has since become a multi-party democracy. The government enacted a policy of national reconciliation and ordered amnesty for those who fought on either side of the war.

In Rhodesia, two armed groups—the Zimbabwe African National Liberation Army (ZANLA) and the Zimbabwe People's Revolutionary Army (ZIPRA) fought against the White government headed by Ian Smith. Rhodesian forces prevailed in the field but were unable to eliminate rebel bases in Mozambique and Zambia, and faced with international sanctions, the government in 1979 agreed to allow universal suffrage. This led to the election of Bishop Abel Muzorewa and the renaming of the country as Rhodesia-Zimbabwe. However, the various factions competed for power, and war continued until 1980 when ZANLA leader Robert Mugabe was elected prime minister and the country was renamed Zimbabwe.

South Africa, feeling threatened by Black liberation movements in the neighboring countries, increased raids against rebel bases in Angola and Zambia through the 1970s and '80s. Internally, the White-ruled government and its policy of apartheid were opposed by the communist-oriented African National Congress (ANC) and the Pan-Africanist Congress (PAC). Both parties were banned in the 1960s, and ANC activist Nelson Mandela was jailed. The military wing of the ANC carried out acts of sabotage and attack on military and police through the 1980s. Bowing to internal and international pressure, the White-minority government abolished all apartheid laws in 1991 and released Nelson Mandela from prison. Multi-party elections were held in 1994, leading to the election of Mandela as president. Mandela promoted a policy of national reconciliation and redistribution of land.

The much-feared slaughter of White citizens never occurred.

Acknowledgments

First off, I would like to thank Mukwae Wabei Siyolwe for her expert editing and advice. I met Mukwae by chance at the very moment I was looking for an African native to review my manuscript with respect to historical and cultural accuracy. Mukwae is Princess Wabei of Barotseland, a region that covers much of the pre-colonial borders of Angola, Namibia, Botswana, Zambia, and Zimbabwe—the region where this story takes place. Mukwae also serves as Chairperson General of the Barotse National Freedom Alliance. Her familiarity with the area's history, the tribes (Black and White), and their mannerisms and figures of speech was invaluable. Thanks also to editor Kyle McCord of Atmosphere Press for his ideas regarding "the big picture," and to Anna Jean Mayhew for spotting everything from misplaced commas to crossed storylines. Helen Bryce, thank you for your suggestions on how to keep my characters real, and Peter Griesinger for stressing the importance of describing the political scene in southern Africa. Finally, thanks to my wife, Cathy Murphy, for proofreading the final copy.

A Brief History of the Giant Sable Antelope

The giant sable antelope (*Hippotragus niger variani*) is a subspecies of the sable antelope and is found only in the forests of Central Angola. It is distinguished from the common sable, which ranges throughout central Africa, by its larger size and, in particular, its enormous curved horns, which can reach a length of up to 65 inches—more than 5 feet.

The giant sable is believed to have branched off from the common sable about 170,000 years ago and remained isolated thereafter in the area between the Cuango and Luando rivers in Angola. Its numbers were never large, and dwindled to an estimated one hundred animals during the 27-year-long Angolan civil war. With its territory now largely protected in the Cangandala National Park and Luanda Nature Reserve, the population has climbed to approximately three hundred animals. It remains on the International Union for Conservation of Nature's (IUCN's) "red list" of critically endangered species.

The giant sable is the national symbol of Angola. Long before that country's independence in 1975, the antelope was revered by local tribes for its beauty, speed, and visual acuity. Africans reportedly sought to protect the animal from European trophy hunters, with the result that the giant sable was unknown to foreigners until the twentieth century.

The first film of the giant sable antelope is believed to have been shot in 1954 by Quentin Keynes, the English adventurer on whom the character of Cecil Covington is based. Keynes was able to approach two bulls engaged in combat and capture their twenty-minute-long fight on his 16mm Bolex camera. In 2002, a year before his death, Keynes was invited to present his film to members of the Explorer's Club in New York City from whom he received a round of applause.

About Atmosphere Press

Founded in 2015, Atmosphere Press was built on the principles of Honesty, Transparency, Professionalism, Kindness, and Making Your Book Awesome. As an ethical and author-friendly hybrid press, we stay true to that founding mission today.

If you're a reader, enter our giveaway for a free book here:

SCAN TO ENTER
BOOK GIVEAWAY

If you're a writer, submit your manuscript for consideration here:

SCAN TO SUBMIT
MANUSCRIPT

And always feel free to visit Atmosphere Press and our authors online at atmospherepress.com. See you there soon!

About the Author

JOHN MANUEL grew up in Gates Mills, Ohio, and graduated from Yale University and the University of North Carolina at Chapel Hill. He now lives in Durham, North Carolina, with his wife, Cathy Murphy. John has published a memoir, *The Canoeist* (Jefferson Press), and three novels—*Hope Valley* (Red Lodge Press), *The Lower Canyons* (Atmosphere Press), and *Solitario* (Atmosphere Press). For more information on John's writing, see *www.jsmanuel.com*.